A Most Improper Duchess

The Three Graces
Book 1

Alanna Lucas

ARE YOU SIGNED UP FOR DRAGONBLADE'S BLOG?

You'll get the latest news and information on exclusive giveaways, exclusive excerpts, coming releases, sales, free books, cover reveals and more.

Check out our complete list of authors, too!

No spam, no junk. That's a promise!

Sign Up Here

www.dragonbladepublishing.com

Dearest Reader;

Thank you for your support of a small press. At Dragonblade Publishing, we strive to bring you the highest quality Historical Romance from some of the best authors in the business. Without your support, there is no 'us', so we sincerely hope you adore these stories and find some new favorite authors along the way.

Happy Reading!

CEO, Dragonblade Publishing

Additional Dragonblade books by Author Alanna Lucas

The Three Graces Series
A Most Improper Duchess (Book 1)

The Lyon's Den Series
How to Steal a Lyon's Fortune

Chapter One

I T WAS WITH a heavy heart that Alexandra and her two sisters were leaving Charis Hall for London. They'd known this day was coming, and yet it was still difficult to accept that this was to be their last day in their home. It was now their sister-in-law's house, as Rachel—Lady Grace as she preferred to be called, even by family—had made perfectly clear upon her arrival less than a week ago.

Since Alexandra and her sisters were now out of mourning after their father's death, Harold, their brother, had informed them upon his arrival that it was time to get on with their lives and marry. The sisters suspected Rachel was behind this not-so-subtle nudging. Their brother had never expressed such sentiments previously. Later that same day, their suspicions were confirmed when his wife had also informed them it was *well past* that time. None of them—including her brother, Alexandra suspected—cared for Rachel. Unfortunately, it was only after Rachel had married Harold that she'd revealed her true conniving and insincere self, and it had worsened with their parents' illnesses.

Rachel had been none too pleased that the girls had vowed to stay with their parents as they had battled through illness rather than each having a London Season, marrying, and moving away.

And then that awful day had come when Mama could no longer fight, and she'd slipped quietly away to Heaven. That had been the beginning of a few devastating years when Papa had not been able discern anymore between reality and the life he'd once known with his love.

It was not long after their mother had died that Harold had informed Rachel that his sire and three sisters would not leave Charis for one of their smaller properties—as she wished—and she would just have to accept that as his final answer. It was the only time he had ever stood up to his domineering wife. Of course, his sisters suspected that Harold had been paying the price each and every day since he'd put his foot down. But the time had come when Harold could no longer put off his pestering wife, and he had finally acquiesced to her demands.

Holding true to form, upon her arrival last week from their estate near Cheltenham, Rachel had swooped in, playing the grieving daughter-in-law who missed her husband's parents, but all the while counting the silver and days until the sisters departed for London. Thankfully, Rachel was making herself scarce today, this last at Charis.

Alexandra and her sisters spent the morning strolling through the immense house, remembering all the fond times they'd shared as a family. The ballroom had always been Alexandra's favorite room. She remembered the last celebration held there as if it were yesterday. It had been such a beautiful evening, celebrating her mother's birthday with family, her parents dancing through the room, the love they shared for each other shining bright in their eyes. It had been a perfect moment in time.

But then their joy had been ripped from them, piece by piece. First, their grandmother had passed away, then Mother had suffered through illness for five years while Father had watched, his mind slowly slipping further and further away from reality. After Mother had died, Father hadn't been able to accept that the love of his life was gone. He'd wandered the halls, talking to her as if she were strolling next to him. In his moments of clarity,

Alexandra and her sisters had tried to explain what had happened, but it was as if he was hearing of his beloved wife's passing for the first time and he grieved all over again. After the second time of watching their sire endure such heartache, the girls had decided to quit revealing the truth to him, and over the course of the following few years they'd become quite creative with their stories as to why Mother was not at home.

Alexandra suspected, however, their father had always known the truth in his heart, for there was such a sadness about him. He'd detested being alone, and so the sisters had taken turns at being by their dear sire's side through the brightest of days and the darkest of the night hours, when the demons in his head had tormented him and his only relief was long walks. Three years had passed before he'd finally found peace and was reunited with his love.

At the end of their stroll through the house, Alexandra left her sisters, wanting a moment to enjoy one of her favorite haunts on the estate one last time. This had been her home—the only one she'd ever known—for four and twenty years. In fact, each of them needed to say their goodbyes alone to the home they'd loved so much. They would have plenty of time to talk in the carriage, share stories and memories, and plan for the Season. Harold had agreed to pay for one Season for the three of them, but she highly doubted that true love could be found and secured with one Season in London for each of the three sisters. Thankfully, once Aunt Imogene heard of Harold's insistence, she informed the girls—in confidence—that she would fund further Seasons. She'd told them that their dearest Mama had wanted them to marry for love, and she would aid them in that quest.

Indeed, one of Alexandra's fondest dreams was to have a large happy family with a man she loved by her side. She would not settle for anything less. Of that much she was sure.

The already cold air chilled even further as she went farther from the house, reminding her that spring had not yet come. The cold never bothered her, or her sisters for that matter—they'd always found beauty in nature regardless of time of year or temperature.

But the day was also grim and dark and was a perfect complement to her current mood. She wandered toward the maze, hoping to escape for a little while within its tall green hedges. In there, she did not have to worry about being spied upon from the house, and she could lose herself to recollections of being a small child chased by her father, laughter echoing all around. She could also give herself to the tears that seemed to be threatening her resolve too much of late.

A cool breeze rustled through the trees, followed by a familiar voice that disrupted her senses. "I thought I might find you here," Niall, the Duke of Blackburn, said as he strolled toward her. "I still remember the first time I rescued you from the evil clutches of this maze."

"I hadn't realized my situation was so dire," she chuckled. Niall always seemed to know what to say to bring a smile to her face. Besides her sisters, he was her dearest friend. Without fail, he'd always been there for her, offering friendship, kindness, and understanding.

"Oh, it was," he said as he took a step closer, his deep voice soothing her troubled soul.

A strange sensation tickled her insides. *It couldn't have anything to do with the nearness of him, could it?* Of course not. She must simply be more emotional about leaving her home than she'd realized. After all, Niall was her oldest friend *and* promised to Lady Nerissa.

She nodded her head and gave a slight curtsey. "Well then, I thank you for that service all those years ago and promise to do my best not to cause too much trouble in the future."

"That is very kind of you," he began, his green eyes teasing, "especially considering your brother has tasked me with seeing you and your sisters safely to London."

Shock caused her words to lodge in her throat. "H . . . Harold is not coming with us?" The sisters missed the person their brother had once been, the fun and playful banter they'd shared with him. Ever since he'd married Rachel, he'd not been the same. She knew her sister-in-law wouldn't be traveling with them, but the sisters had assumed their brother would make the journey and spend at least a few days with them while they settled in at Great-aunt Imogene's. They had hoped it might be enough to draw him back to his former self. "When did this happen?"

"On our ride this morning." The spot between his brows crinkled. "He didn't tell you?"

"My brother has become a great one for secrets. He does not tell anything of his thoughts. I suspect he is not . . ." She clasped her lips tight. It was one thing for her and her sisters to complain about their sister-in-law in private and quite another to gossip about her. Despite Rachel's unpleasantness, Alexandra would not give in to bitterness.

"You needn't say more." Niall's eyes softened with understanding. "All our friends have noticed the difference in him, and it only gets worse with each passing year."

"I miss the brother he once was." The thought of how close they'd been with their brother and how distant he now was tore at her heart.

"Perhaps his being here amongst all the memories you shared while growing up will bring him back."

Alexandra shook her head, knowing very well her sister-in-law would not allow Harold to reminisce about his time before her, even in his own head. "It is her home now."

"It may be her house now, but she is not the keeper of your— or his—memories, of all the wonderful times you spent here. You will always have those."

"That's something Papa would have said. I wish he were still here," she ended in a whisper, quickly looking away in an attempt to hide the tears pooling in her eyes.

She felt Niall step closer, and then he spoke and it was her undoing. "I am here for you . . . always."

The tears she'd only barely managed to keep at bay stormed down her cheeks, and in the next breath, he was at her side, holding her, comforting her, just as he had done when her mother, then her dearest Papa, had died.

A large, gentle, soothing hand held her close. "It's all right, Alex, just let it all out."

With the mention of his pet name for her—one that she had not cared for at first—a giggle escaped her lips. "You do have a way with words, Your Grace," she sniffled. He detested use of the honorific just as much as she once had Alex, but in the past few years, something had shifted between them and now she didn't mind the name. She supposed it was because they were such good friends. For as long as she could remember, Niall had always made her feel safe.

His words were soft yet reassuring. "You and your sisters have dealt with the changes and grief remarkably well. I know it has not been easy for any of you."

She rubbed her cheek against his chest, relishing in the strength that surrounded her. "Thank you. That means a great deal, especially coming from you." She was close with her sisters, but Niall had become her rock during the darkest hours when each sister had tried to cope with the stress and loss in her own way. Evelina had taken to poetry. Theodora—the youngest—when not wandering, could be found at the pianoforte at all hours of the day and night.

What would she do without Niall when he married Lady Nerissa? Would they still maintain such a close friendship? Her heart constricted as the pain of uncertainty wrapped around it. There were too many changes lurking on the horizon. She raised her cheek from his chest, looking past her reflection in his spectacles and into his green eyes. Time stood still for a brief moment, her breath catching as warmth filled her heart and something foreign passed between them.

Confusion laced her thoughts as she tried to reason with what she was feeling. *What could . . . could it be . . . no. It's nothing. I'm just overly tired and emotional from everything that has happened.*

"I . . . I think I should return to the house. We have an early start tomorrow and I still have some packing to complete."

Niall cleared his throat, taking a step back and offering his arm. And once again, he took away her worries with playful words. "I certainly hope that you leave your breeches behind." Whether roaming the grounds or riding her horse, Alexandra had always very much enjoyed the freedom she felt when wearing trousers. "It would be very improper for you to be seen wearing them in Town."

"I know," she responded with a sly smile.

A single brown brow raised in concern.

She would never do anything too shocking or improper, but it was still fun to tease her dearest friend just the same.

THE NEXT MORNING, the Grace sisters, along with Niall, his sister, and the Dowager Duchess of Blackburn, departed for London. Thankfully, the dowager rode in her own conveyance with her children, leaving Alexandra and her sisters blissfully alone in the carriage provided by their brother. The dowager scowled far too much for Alexandra's liking. She truly did not know how Niall and his youngest sister, Naomi, tolerated her sourness for any length of time.

Alexandra watched the lush green countryside pass them by. There had been so many additional preparations as of late, she hadn't stopped to take in the beauty that was early spring, and the renewal and hope it brought. Closing her eyes, she inhaled deeply, then slowly exhaled, releasing the tension. Their parents would not have wanted them to dwell on the sorrow and heartache of the last eight years. Quite the contrary. They would have wanted the girls to rise above it and live life to the fullest. She was determined to honor their spirit. She took in another deep breath, filling her lungs with the crisp morning air. This was the beginning of a new adventure for the Grace sisters.

"I'm thinking about them, as well," Theodora said.

"Me, too," Evelina, who was the second eldest of the Grace sisters, chimed in. "Will the pain ever go away?"

"With time I suspect it will," Alexandra said, trying to convince herself as well as her sisters. "Mama and Papa would want us to enjoy the Season."

At four and twenty, she was embarking on her first Season, along with her two sisters. Evelina was two and twenty and Theodora had recently turned one and twenty. They knew they were considered old by *ton* standards to only just be entering Society. But despite what some of the gossips would say, the girls believed they were prepared to enter Society with grace and determination. They would not be swayed by others' opinions of them.

"Do you think Aunt Imogene is prepared to chaperone all three of us?" Theodora asked.

"Based on her enthusiasm in her last letter, I believe she is very much looking forward to having us in residence," Evelina assured their younger sister.

Their elderly aunt had been briefly married once nearly fifty years ago and was considered quite eccentric by the *ton*, but the girls adored her. Aunt Imogene seemed to dance to her own tune, never caring what others thought of her. Of course, when one's wealth rivalled that of Croesus, it was easier to shun Society's rules. Without a doubt, Theodora was taking after their dearest relation.

"I think it would be best if you didn't wear Papa's coat while in Town, Theodora," Alexandra gently suggested. It was her youngest sister's favorite keepsake of their papa's. She'd taken Father's death the hardest. Despite frequently being unable to remember that Theodora was his daughter, they'd grown extremely close, and over the course of his illness she'd grown most protective of him, hardly ever leaving his side. She'd been his constant companion on his nightly strolls.

Theodora pulled the edges of the coat closer about her. "I will not wear it to social events, but that is all that I can promise," she conceded. "What are the chances that I could make a match, marry, and return to the country in less than a fortnight?"

"Very slim, and besides, we agreed we would help each other through our first Season." Alexandra did not want to think about the day when each of them would be married with families of their own and living apart from one another. The three Grace sisters had always been together.

Truth be told, she was a little worried. Oh, she knew she and her sisters would always be close regardless of distance, but it felt as if with each breath she took there were more changes storming onto the horizon. One thing was certain, though. She would not settle for an advantageous marriage purely because that was what was expected of her as the daughter of a viscount. She was determined to marry for love. She wished for a husband who would treat her just as Niall had, only with the addition of that all-important passion.

The problem was she didn't know how to go about finding such a man. Hopefully the Season would reveal him to her.

The hours passed in pleasant conversation, the sisters discussing their hopes for the Season. By the end of their first day of travel, they were all tired but feeling optimistic about the future.

Before too long, they were at the first overnight stop of their journey. The carriage door opened, revealing a hazy sunset. Alexandra stepped down, followed by her sisters, and glanced about the traveling inn's stable yard when Niall strolled toward them.

"I hope this leg of the journey wasn't too uncomfortable for you all? The recent rains made for an uneven ride."

Before Alexandra could respond, Naomi playfully scolded, "Oh, Niall, must you always be so formal all the time?" She turned to the three Graces. "This is most exciting, all of us having our first Season together." At eighteen, Naomi was quite enthusiastic about being out in Society, whereas the sisters were more prudent. That wasn't to say they didn't want to have fun, but they were more interested in musicales and other intellectual diversions than crowded ballrooms and the latest *on dits*.

"That is quite enough, Naomi," Her Grace, the Dowager Duchess of Blackburn, reprimanded as she exited her conveyance, joining them. "We need our rest for tackling the remainder of the journey." And with that, the duchess practically pushed her daughter away from them. Not for the first time, Alexandra wondered how Naomi stayed so cheerful with a mother such as this.

"I apologize for—"

"There's no need," Alexandra reassured Niall. For reasons she could not explain, despite being neighbors in the country, the duchess had never seemed to care for Alexandra and her sisters. "I suppose we should get settled before supper." She offered a smile and went to her sisters.

An hour later, the sisters gathered in a private parlor for an evening meal. Niall strolled into the room looking handsome in his simple evening attire. There was something different about him, something that demanded Alexandra's attention.

Yes, he is handsome, but Niall is just your friend. Too many thoughts were clouding her mind.

Besides, she'd never much thought of him in that way before. Why would she think him handsome now? Though she had to admit he was without a doubt the most intelligent gentleman of her acquaintance. If he were a woman, he would be labeled a bluestocking. Really, his only negative trait was that he was quite aloof at social gatherings.

A sadness swept over her. *And he is promised to Lady Nerissa.*

Just then she met his gaze and their eyes locked for one brief moment before Theodora's question broke through the moment. "Is Naomi not joining us?"

Niall cleared his throat and turned his attention to her sister as if nothing had transpired between them. Perhaps it had all been in her imagination.

"My mother has decided that she and my sister will take trays in their room then rest for the remainder of the evening." She could hear the sarcasm in Niall's voice and knew he was thinking the same. *The only rest Naomi needs is from her mother.* "Hopefully, once in London, my mother won't dictate my sister's actions as much."

No sooner had the words left his mouth than they all burst into laughter.

"I don't think that is possible," Theodora blurted.

"I don't either," Niall started as he pushed the spectacles up his nose. "The entire way here, all Mother talked about was Naomi's list of events."

"That's probably why they needed to rest," Alexandra quipped.

A simple fare was laid before them and the party of four dined, continuing with their conversation.

"Since I am to keep an eye on the Grace sisters, what is your plan for the Season?"

Out of the corner of her eye, Alexandra spied her sisters watching her closely. What were they up to? *Just ignore them*, she inwardly shook her head.

"We have left the planning to Aunt Imogene," she offered.

"I'm certain there won't be a dull moment," he jested. Although their days and evenings were certain to be quite full, Alexandra wondered just how much excitement Town could offer. They'd ventured to London once in the early days of their mother's illness so that she could consult with a specialist, but none of them had found the excursion exciting or even remotely entertaining.

The evening passed with pleasant conversation and much laughter, but they had all planned to set out early the next morning, so before too long, Alexandra and her sisters were ensconced in their room. All Alexandra wanted to do was slip under the covers and sleep peacefully, but her sisters had other ideas. She had only just managed to sit on her bed when the interrogation began.

"What was all that about?" Evelina tilted her head, her eyes wide as she waited for Alexandra to answer.

"What was all what about?" Alexandra huffed out as she fluffed up her pillow, not knowing what her sister meant.

Both her siblings eyed her for several seconds before Theodora finally spoke. "You know we know, but if you're not ready to confess your feelings for a certain gentleman then Evelina and I will simply wait."

Theodora could not be insinuating she had feelings for Niall? He was her best friend and confidant. And besides, there was no passion or spark between them. The whole idea was simply preposterous. She turned up her nose and replied, "I truly do not know what the two of you are referring to."

"Perhaps she doesn't," Evelina stated, her eyes narrowing with disbelief as she stared at her older sister, as if trying to see deep into her soul. Evelina could be so tiresome at times.

"Then we should not tell her." Theodora nudged Evelina. "It will be great fun to watch it unfold."

"Watch what unfold?" Alexandra demanded as she crossed her arms.

The only thing they would ever see were two friends, but clearly their imaginations were getting the better of them this evening and vexing Alexandra in the process. She could never entertain thoughts of Niall. He had been promised to Lady Nerissa ever since the dowager duchess had concocted *the scheme*, as Niall referred to it. Not that Evelina or Theodora knew anything about the scheme. Very few did.

"Nothing." Her two sisters caroled in unison.

Alexandra chose to ignore them and instead nestled under the covers, pulling the blanket up over her head as sounds of their giggles permeated through the material.

Chapter Two

SILENCE ENVELOPED THE gently swaying carriage, allowing Niall to reflect on the past days. Why he had ever agreed to watch over the Grace sisters was beyond him. He did his best to hide his feelings for Alexandra, but every so often, she did something that stirred his desire anew, and his resolve was tested again.

When he was a young lad, the prospect of marrying a friend of the family had not seemed so daunting—at the tender age of ten, he hadn't fully understood what it even meant to be promised to Lady Nerissa. But that had shifted as he aged.

After Father passed, he'd approached his mother on a couple of occasions in an attempt to avoid marrying Lady Nerissa, but his pleas had fallen on deaf ears. Mother had even enlisted the aid of his older sisters to talk some sense into him. It had never been a pleasant conversation, and it was one he did not want repeated . . . again. So he'd stamped down his emotions and committed to doing his duty. He'd studied hard, made improvements to their estates, ensured his three siblings received an education suitable for sisters of a duke, taken care of family matters, and . . . withered inside. If it hadn't been for his interest in books on architecture, landscape design, and Greek mythology, he would have gone mad.

By the time he'd entered his early twenties, a fair young lady was catching his attention as well. She had such *joie de vivre*, even in the face of uncertainty and tragedy.

He still remembered with precise clarity the day his feelings for Alexandra shifted into something more than just friendship. After enduring yet another lecture from his mother, he'd embarked on a long walk. Why he'd ventured toward Charis Hall he could not remember, but when he'd reached the maze and heard soft crying, his heart had ached. And when he'd found Alexandra, arms wrapped around herself, trying to find solace, his heart had nearly broken. Without thought for propriety, he went to her and held her.

She'd confided her fears over her mother's declining health, and they'd talked for hours, each sharing their fears and innermost thoughts. Something had shifted on that distant day—at least for him—but he knew he could never act on what he felt.

His mother had made certain of that.

For as long as he could remember, she had constantly reminded him of his promised nuptials, not to mention what was expected of him as a duke. As if he could ever forget the latter. The duties of the dukedom, thrust upon him at an early age, had consumed him. He'd spent so much time doing service for others that now, at seven and twenty, he felt as if life was passing him by.

"You're awfully quiet," his mother stated matter-of-factly. Niall met her gaze, the harshness in her eyes telling him she wasn't pleased. A moment later, she unleashed her fury. "I hope you are not considering abandoning your responsibilities while in Town and—"

"Mother," he broke across what was sure to be a well-rehearsed and familiar tirade. "I have never abandoned anything. Stop comparing me to Father. I know my duties and I am prepared to see them through. This is the last time I will have this conversation with you." He hadn't meant to sound quite so firm, but the constant nagging was wearing on him. He was nothing like his sire. His mama made certain that any resemblance was swiftly eradicated. And besides, he'd hardly known the man who had died when Niall was twelve.

His statement seemed to appease her for now. She simply offered a half-smile, then turned her attention to the passing countryside. If not for the issue with his horse's shoe, he would be riding alongside the conveyance, rather than being cooped up with his mother and youngest sister, who, despite having slumbered all night, was currently sound asleep and thankfully had not witnessed the disagreement.

Silence, blissful silence, once again filled the carriage, allowing him to escape into his own musings. He had been designing a renovation and refacing of his home near Doncaster. He'd created dozens of sketches but had yet to finalize the design, and then there was the surrounding landscape to be tackled. He was equally enthusiastic about creating a complimentary outlook. He'd always enjoyed spending time in the country and hoped his future bride would share his passion as well.

The hours passed, and before long, they were creeping their way through London at a slow pace. It seemed as if every family from the *ton* had chosen that day to return from the country. It was going to be a tiring Season indeed.

AFTER AN EXHAUSTING journey, the Grace sisters finally entered London, and their party parted ways with Niall's as they neared their aunt's home. Before long, their carriage came to a gentle halt, and Alexandra could hear dear Great-aunt Imogene's exuberant voice. By the time the steps had been prepared and the sisters handed down, Aunt Imogene was at their sides patting their cheeks and squeezing their hands.

"I thought you would never arrive." She grabbed Theodora's hand, then motioned for Alexandra and Evelina to follow. "Your rooms have been readied. We are to have dinner at home tonight. Tomorrow, we are to go to Lady Tassell's musicale. It will not be a grand affair, but it will be an excellent event to start the Season on the right foot. Her daughters are quite accomplished and I'm certain you will find the entertainment most pleasing. Lord Redford and Mr. Hewlett are to be in attendance. They are both considered extremely eligible and I'm sure they will be most sought after this Season. Oh, I almost forgot Mr. Fuller. He is a great lover of music as well."

Alexandra wondered when their aunt would take a breath. Even after they entered the house, she continued to prattle on and on about the Season, which of its events were the most sought after, the girls' competition, and which gentlemen should be avoided. Only once they reached their rooms did she pause.

"Take your time getting settled. I will see you downstairs in about an hour and we can get all caught up." And with that, Aunt Imogene took her leave.

Alexandra wanted to state that taking one's time usually meant a more relaxed pace and not having such precise arrangements to follow, but she was keen to spend time with her aunt, too.

"I didn't think she would ever stop talking," Theodora giggled. "For a woman of two and seventy, she certainly is spry. How are we ever to keep up with her?"

"I'm sure she's just excited to have us finally in residence," Alexandra smiled. Mother had once told her that Aunt Imogene wanted children but not a husband. And since one could not respectably have the first without the latter, Aunt Imogene had married. But it wasn't a love match, and when her husband of only six months had died after taking a nasty fall from his horse, she'd declared that she did not care for the union and would not remarry. She'd held fast to that declaration and decided instead to dote on her nieces and nephews, and then great-nieces and -nephew, for the rest of her life.

"Aunt Imogene so loves having people around her. I've always wondered what she disliked about having a husband," Theodora said. Their youngest sister had always expressed her desire to marry and have a family. They all had.

"I truly don't know." Alexandra inwardly sighed. None of them were prepared for this new adventure of husband hunting. And worse, she herself did not want to hunt; she wanted to fall head over heels in love.

"Father was a husband, and Mother never complained," Theodora reasoned. "And I cannot recall hearing Grandmama state any aversion to marriage or a husband, either." She paused for a long moment, then questioned, "Do you think Aunt Imogene's husband was an unkind man?"

The girls were not entirely sheltered from the ways of the world and had heard stories from one of the local country girls, who'd once told them that her father ruled the house with a heavy hand.

"It is something we should not ask. If Aunt Imogene wants us to know, she will discuss it in her own time," Evelina stated with practicality. Although she was creative and curious, she was in possession of the most common sense.

"I suppose you are correct." Worry lines creased Theodora's forehead, but before Alexandra could ask what was troubling her youngest sister, she blurted out her woes. "How are we to know the true nature of men?"

Silence enveloped them, each lost in the question posed. It was a troubling one at that. Their knowledge of the opposite sex was limited.

You know Niall.

True, but he is a friend, nothing more.

"I suppose all we can do is observe them at social gatherings, pay heed to any gossip, and rely on instinct," Evelina offered. "As long as we stick together, all will be well. And once one of us makes a match, she can enlighten the rest."

Alexandra certainly hoped so.

ALEXANDRA AND HER sisters had been in Town for four days and had already attended two dinner parties, a musicale, and endured a shopping expedition and countless visits to numerous friends of their great-aunt's acquaintance. But tonight marked their first ball. They were all equally excited. Oh, for certain, they'd attended country dances and dinner parties, but this was their first ball *in London.*

After being announced, Alexandra and her two sisters walked into the opulent ballroom behind Aunt Imogene. Candlelight danced across the vast walls as dozens of couples meticulously performed the quadrille. There was an air of eagerness that wafted through the room. It appeared that everyone wanted to impress this evening, to begin the Season in a positive way.

Opening her fan with a flick of her wrist, Aunt Imogene leaned in and uttered, "There's Lord Redford. Oh, and there's Lord Kirkwood. It would appear that some of the most eligible gentlemen are present this evening." She then tsked a couple of times and added, "And several who are quite ineligible."

On the surface, the gentlemen present appeared the same. What made one man eligible and another not? Were wealth and title factors or something else altogether? Alexandra suspected Society's standards when it came to a good match was vastly different from her own—or that of her sisters. And, what of the gossip? It would seem that the tiniest hint of scandal, whether true or not, could harm one's reputation. How would they discover their answers?

Too lost in thought, she hadn't noticed a rather tall gentleman approach their trio. Aunt Imogene whispered from behind her fan, "That is Lord Dougherty. He is a rake and—Oh, Lord Dougherty, how pleasant to see you this evening. I trust your mother is feeling better." Their aunt's vibrant voice rose above the chatter in the ballroom.

"Much better, Lady Middleton, thank you. I believe the doctor was overly concerned. She is presently in Bath." Lord Dougherty eyed the sisters with interest, his roving gaze quite unsettling. Alexandra definitely put him in the ineligible category.

"Allow me to introduce my nieces." Aunt Imogene pointed her fan as she said their names. "Miss Grace, Miss Evelina, and Miss Theodora."

He performed an elegant bow, one that Alexandra suspected he'd practiced at length in front of a looking glass. "Now that we have been properly introduced. Miss Evelina, would you do me the honor of accepting the next dance."

If Evelina objected to Lord Dougherty's request—as Alexandra suspected she did—she did not let on. They had been well-trained for this Season. Her sister pasted on a pleasant smile and accepted his hand.

Once out of earshot, Aunt Imogene informed the remaining two sisters of Lord Dougherty's circumstances. "He is a known rake, which isn't necessarily bad *if* the rake in question can be reformed. However, that is not his only known vice. He is a compulsive gambler and is rumored to be in a considerable amount of debt."

"So, he is a fortune hunter?" Alexandra questioned as she watched Evelina dance with the rake. His movements were elegant and practiced. She could see how a young lady could fall victim to his charms, although perhaps one should not judge solely based on outward appearances. Just then, a pleasant laugh from a neighboring group of ladies caught her attention. She turned and noticed a beautiful young lady—though her dress was unfashionable and her countenance shy and unsure—standing with an older woman who seemed just as awkward. "Do you know who the lady in cream is, Aunt Imogene?" she whispered.

Her aunt followed Alexandra's gaze. "That is Miss Samuels. Her family has no funds for entertainments such as these, and so her aunt is aiding this Season. It is such a shame, too." Aunt Imogene tsked again several times. "She is such an agreeable young lady and has such a beautiful singing voice. She is fortunate her aunt is in a position to support her."

As if sensing the conversation was about them, the older woman and Miss Samuels moved toward them.

Aunt Imogene greeted her friend with much enthusiasm. "Mrs. Samuels, such a pleasure to see you this evening. It's been too long since our last meeting."

"Indeed, it has. I have been much consumed with preparing my niece for the Season." Mrs. Samuels waved a hand and with a warm, caring smile said, "Oh, I almost forgot my manners. Allow me to introduce Miss Samuels."

After brief acknowledgments, the girls moved to one side, allowing their aunts to discuss the latest *on dits*. Although Aunt Imogene had professed numerous times that she did not care for gossip, she'd also informed the sisters that it was vital to know what went on within the *ton*. Alexandra supposed that included *on dits*.

"I understand you enjoy singing?" Theodora, the most musically inclined of the three sisters, asked.

"Yes," Miss Samuels answered shyly. "I also enjoy playing the pianoforte and the harp as well. My aunt has a beautiful pianoforte at her house, and it has been such a pleasure, spending hours practicing." As she continued to talk about singing and music her countenance brightened, and her passion shone through.

"Do you practice every day?"

"Oh yes. And when I am not practicing, I'm thinking about music. It's as if music is part of my soul." She let out a giggle. "That must sound rather silly."

"On the contrary, I feel the same," Theodora offered. "You must join us tomorrow at our salon. It is very informal, and we discuss all sorts of topics, including music."

"I would be most honored," Miss Samuels said as her head dipped slightly in that shy way.

"Oh, there is Naomi," Theodora started. "I must introduce you to her. She is not musically inclined but has an excellent ear. I think you'll find her most agreeable. And she's with Miss Ashton, who you must meet as well." She turned to Alexandra. "You don't mind?"

"Not at all." As Theodora led Miss Samuels away, Alexandra suspected that the two girls were at the start of a true friendship— at least she hoped so.

A moment later, her aunt said, "Oh, and there is Lady Lamden. You'll be fine on your own for a few moments, won't you?" Aunt Imogene didn't wait for an answer before scurrying off with Mrs. Samuels toward their friend. And with that, Alexandra was left alone to take in everything swirling about her.

It was not as if she was entirely unpracticed in the ways of the *ton*. During the early years of their mother's illness, they had ventured to Bath so that she could take the waters. But after that, as Mother's health had declined, they'd kept mostly to the country, enjoying local balls and assemblies. However, those events paled in comparison to the grandeur of tonight's enter-tainment. But even after being in Town less than a week, Alexandra had determined that she most definitely preferred the country.

She was scanning the ballroom, watching all the couples perform their rituals for securing a dance partner by attracting attention, or in some cases, trying to avoid it, when from across the room, she spied Niall. Her heart gave a little lurch. Even from this distance, she could sense he was uncomfortable, unsettled even, and in need of a friend.

For reasons she could not explain, she felt a strong desire to go to him, to ease his troubles. Perhaps it was because he'd always been there for her.

ONE WOULD THINK that after spending several Seasons in London, Niall would be more comfortable at large events. But here he was, more uncomfortable than ever, and trying to disappear into the column beside him.

Worse still, his sister not only seemed to attract attention, but to relish it. He was certain there would be a swarm of eligible and not-so-suitable gentlemen knocking on their door in morning. She was currently dancing with Mr. Rodney, a known gambler in need of a wealthy wife. He inwardly shook his head. This was going to be a *long* Season.

"I see your sister has been cornered by Mr. Rodney. He is not very agreeable," Alexandra said as she edged up to him.

His pulse instantly reacted to the nearness of her. *Don't think about what can never be.* He took in a deep breath to steady his breathing, and focused on his current woes. "I would concur, but Naomi is determined to dance with every gentleman at least once this Season." He let out a long sigh. He wanted Naomi to find a love match, unlike his other sisters, who'd both settled for titles and wealth. They were just like his mother in that regard, and he was most certain they were just as miserable. Someone in his family should marry for love and not duty. Since he knew it would not be him, he was determined to aid his youngest sister in that quest.

"And I see you are determined to become a column at these events," she offered. "Or perhaps a wallflower?"

"Definitely not a wallflower." But he could live with being called a column. "What style of column?" he retorted, bantering playfully.

"Let me think." She tapped her finger against her creamy cheek then a moment later said, "Doric."

Her response took him aback. "Why Doric?"

"Formal, neat and tidy."

"So, I'm dull," he said. He didn't want to be seen as dull or a wallflower, especially not in Alexandra's eyes. Although he was promised to another, he was still a man and preferred not to be seen in such ill light.

"No. Classically understated."

"Classically understated?" He thought for a moment. That was better than being called dull. "I'm satisfied."

"I'm glad." She flashed one of her beautiful smiles that always made his heart flutter. "Now that that's settled, will you do me the honor of the next dance, Your Grace?"

"It is quite scandalous and most improper of you to ask," he began as he leaned in and whispered, "Alex." Whenever Alexandra was near, he was more relaxed, more confident.

He offered his arm and led her to the floor. It felt natural to be next to her, as if they were meant to be side by side.

Across the room, he spied the woman he was promised to, speaking with Miss Raine. A pang of guilt struck his heart. *Lady Nerissa.*

He had nothing against the debutante, but she was not his choice of bride, and he did not believe he was her first choice of husband. Their parents had concocted the plan years ago. Thankfully, only their mutual families knew of the arrangement—and Alexandra of course. There was very little he kept from her.

Only your feelings for her.

He had to.

As Lady Nerissa's eighteenth birthday had neared, she'd begged her parents for a Season, and thankfully, they'd acquiesced. He would honor the promise because that was who he was, but if Lady Nerissa fell in love *and* somehow convinced her parents—not to mention his mother—to annul the promise, then he would gladly call it off. And if not . . . he would simply enjoy these moments with Alexandra.

"It would seem you asked me for a waltz," he whispered as they took their places.

Since the Prince Regent included the waltz at a ball last year, Niall had only waltzed on one other occasion but not with anyone he cared about. He'd never noticed how intimate the dance was before now. As they moved through the elegant turns, he could feel her chest rise and fall, her sweet breath tickling his senses.

He wondered if she'd ever felt more for him than just friendship?

Why would the beautiful and accomplished, amusing and vibrant Alexandra be interested in a man who enjoyed the country, reading by the fire, and studying architecture? *Perhaps . . .*

He shook that thought away. *There was no perhaps*, he had to keep reminding himself. His sole purpose in coming to Town, other than the usual obligations of a duke, was to chaperone his sister, not torture himself over impossibilities. Too many others were in complete control of his fate.

All too soon the dance ended and he was returning Alexandra to her sisters. "Thank you for the dance—"

"There you are," his mother's firm tone rippled down his spine. "It is time to leave. Naomi has made quite the spectacle by dancing with Mr. Norley." His sister's cheeks flamed with embarrassment at their mother's words. Now was not the time or place to question what had occurred. It was best he removed Mother before *she* made a spectacle.

He said his farewells and then joined his mother and Naomi as they promptly and efficiently departed the ballroom.

Once clear of prying ears, he asked his mother, "And what is wrong with Mr. Norley?"

She did not answer, keeping her gaze straight ahead and focused on the exit. The tension and silence continued to rise as they waited for their carriage. Only once ensconced in the ducal conveyance and on their way did she unleash her fury.

"I will tell you *exactly* what is wrong with Mr. Norley." She took in a deep breath then aired her grievance. "He has no title. Your sister is the daughter of a duke. He is the second son of baron. Of a baron!"

Naomi made the mistake of speaking. "But he has property and—"

"He has a small house near Plymouth, if we are to believe

that." The duchess's words dripped with disgust. She then turned her anger on Niall. "If you cannot act in the best interests of the family, then I will—"

"What, Mother? What will you do?" He challenged her. "It was one dance. Leave Naomi be." He gathered his words and put her in her place. "All I do is what is best for this family. Have I not lived up to the ducal title? Have I not come to chaperone my sister despite my dislike of London? Am I not promised to Lady Nerissa? Have I not—"

"I suppose you have acted in an acceptable manner." That was the closest Mother had ever come to a compliment. "And I suppose I can let this evening's indiscretions slide, but Naomi has to promise that she will be more discerning in her choice of dance partners."

Even though the carriage was dark, he could sense that his sister was about to argue, so he quickly interjected. "Naomi will take more care. She and I will discuss it later."

He had no intention of restricting his sister. She would just have to be cleverer in her designs.

By the time they reached their home, both mother and daughter were still fuming but, thankfully, silent.

"I am retiring," was all the duchess said as she walked past them and up the stairs. Niall knew that she expected him to reprimand Naomi, despite the late hour.

The moment he guided his sister to his study and closed the door, the tension that had been gnawing at both of them eased. The room was warm and comfortable, his sanctuary. He moved to the side table and poured a glass of brandy.

"You're not going to make me abide by her demands, are you?"

"No. I want you to be happy." He took a sip of the amber liquid, instantly feeling it burn his throat. "But you *do* have to be more cautious, or neither of us will survive the Season with Mother. I suggest that events where she is in attendance, you are more discerning about your choice of dance partner."

"But she's always—"

"I will see that Mother stays home on a few occasions." He knew it wouldn't be too difficult. He just had to accept invitations to gatherings hosted by ladies of—in the dowager duchess's estimation—lesser standing. She wouldn't be pleased, but that should give his sister the opportunity to enjoy at least a couple of events before their mother caught on to their plan.

Naomi sat down, slipped off her shoes then tucked her feet under her dress. "Do you truly want to marry Lady Nerissa? I mean, she's pleasant, but . . ."

"But what?" He never discussed anything of own personal desires. Had he somehow revealed his feelings for Alexandra?

"You don't seem to suit each other. There, I said it," she finished with a huff.

Niall sat down on the sofa beside her. "No, we don't. Our mothers believe otherwise, though."

"Surely there is something you can do to get out of it. You sacrifice so much for this family, yet you deserve to be happy, too."

If only it were that simple. He was a man of honor. He was expected to do what was best for the dukedom and marry a woman of exceptional lineage, have children—male children— grow the estates, and maintain the legacy that generations of Blackburns had before him. But it was nice that his sibling recognized his efforts.

"Let's focus on your prospects." He truly did not want to dwell on his life.

Naomi shook her head, then offered a sympathetic smile. "You always put everyone before yourself." She leaned over and kissed his cheek. "I am most grateful that you're my brother."

$$\sim \! \! \ast \! \! \sim$$

Chapter Three

THE NEW DAY brought with it all sorts of new experiences. After receiving a dozen gentleman callers—albeit none who caught their fancy—the Grace sisters turned their attention to preparations for their afternoon salon. When they were in the country, some of the happiest, most pleasant afternoons spent were in the presence of friends, talking about their favorite diversions, playing games, and listening to music. They hoped to bring a little of that joy into their aunt's home.

Before too long, the parlor was filled with ladies from the finest families of the *ton*. However, the sisters quickly learned that just because someone belonged to a prestigious family did not mean they were good or kind individuals.

"I want to thank you for inviting me. It is such a pleasure to be included," Miss Samuels said with a warm, bright smile.

"I assure you the pleasure is all ours," Alexandra reassured her as she glanced from one sister to another. "I must admit, we have an ulterior—"

"We hope you won't mind singing for us?" Theodora interrupted, practically begging. "I can accompany you on the pianoforte." Her youngest sister would always gravitate to those who shared her passion for music.

"I would be most honored."

Once the guests had all assembled in the music room, Miss Samuels took her position next to the pianoforte. Theodora's fingers swept across the keys, creating a lovely sound, but as soon as Miss Samuels began to sing, the room quieted, all those present mesmerized by the sweet melody that she caressed from her lips.

Like so many ladies of the *ton*, Alexandra and her sisters were accomplished in the usual diversions. But few attained such a level of perfection as Miss Samuels. As the song came to an end, everyone stood and offered applause and praise.

"Miss Samuels has such a lovely voice," Miss Newman commented to Alexandra. "Such a pity her dowry is so paltry."

"Someone's worth does not lie in the amount of money they have in their purse but in—"

"That is easy for you to say." Miss Newman's harsh retort disrupted the gaiety around them.

Alexandra was stunned. "And what exactly does that mean?" she challenged.

"Money is not a concern for you. You and your sisters want for nothing. You're beautiful and accomplished, well-liked and admired, and have not a care in the world."

Alexandra opened her mouth to speak, but Evelina spoke first. "Life is not perfect for us either. We have had our share of heartache. But we choose to be happy, to find joy amongst ourselves and others."

It was not a secret how long their mother, and then father, had suffered through illness, but some of these chits could only see what was on the surface. Despite their pleasant outward appearances, some of those present truly had the ugliest of souls. And yet, they would be regarded with esteem because of rank, title, and wealth. Would their marriages be any happier than those without funds or title?

"So you say," Miss Newman huffed in an unladylike fashion.

"I do say. And if you cannot grasp that, then I suggest you take your leave." Theodora and Alexandra moved closer to their sister. No one would treat the Grace sisters thusly. They would not tolerate one of their own being degraded in such a way, nor any of their friends. This conversation would likely cause some gossip, but each sister knew the others agreed that taking a stand for friends was worth whatever consequence may come their way.

Miss Newman scanned the room, then with another huff, turned her nose upward and stormed out. A few other ladies followed her almost in a panic, as if they had to choose sides. Alexandra suspected the lady and cronies in question would try to spread some vile gossip, but it was nothing they could not deal with. They had not done anything wrong. They could not help the station to which they'd been born, just as Miss Samuels had had no control over hers. But what they could help—somewhat at least—were the friends they kept.

All were subdued for several minutes, absorbing what had just occurred, when Miss Samuels turned to the sisters. "Thank you for coming to my defense. I know my family doesn't have much to offer in the way of a dowry, and it has been seen as a deficit by many, but I do hope you are correct."

"Any gentleman would be lucky to have you a wife. Never underestimate your worth."

Alexandra knew she would do everything within her reach to aid Miss Samuels in finding a love match and that, without a doubt, her sisters would assist too.

Despite Miss Newman's sourness, the afternoon was a success. Alexandra sensed that those who remained would become true friends. Regardless, she and her sisters would exercise caution in the future. One could never be too careful in situations such as these. They still had to find their own matches, and attracting the notice of the gossips most certainly would not do.

Once their guests had left, the sisters retreated upstairs to their private parlor. It was one of their favorite rooms in the house. It was where they could talk without censure and just be themselves.

"Who do you think will suit Miss Samuels?" Evelina questioned. "I am determined to help her find a match."

"It must be a gentleman not in need of money, who has an interest in music and—"

"What about Lord Jacobs?" An excited gasp burst from Theodora. "Or . . . or Mr. Fuller! I happened to overhear Lady Lamden mention his skills with the violin at the musicale, *and* he is on Aunt Imogene's list."

"Did someone mention my name?" Aunt Imogene said as she entered the room. Her overly innocent countenance suggested she was up to something.

"We were just discussing prospects for Miss Samuels and thought Mr. Fuller would be perfect a match."

"He is quite musically inclined." Their aunt paused for a moment as if recalling all the gentleman's attributes. "Yes, I believe you're quite right. He is not in need of money, so her lack of fortune is not a hindrance, and they would make a lovely pair. And I know he will be attending Lady Kirkwood's dinner party tonight."

"Now all we have to do is come up with a plan." Evelina clasped her hands together as if already plotting.

A moment later, two footmen carrying a large trunk with fanciful scrollwork along the sides entered the room. "Just put it near the sofa. Thank you." Aunt Imogene turned to the girls. "I have a surprise for you. The last time your mother was in London, she mentioned that she thought you girls might enjoy seeing this," she said as the footmen set the trunk down. She opened the lid, revealing numerous decorative boxes in varying sizes and dozens of neatly folded letters.

Evelina removed and opened the letter on top. "It's a love letter from Father. It's dated the year before he and Mother married."

"I never understood why your mother wanted it kept here instead of in her own home, but here we are," Aunt Imogene started. "I will leave you to enjoy your parents' courtship." She ended with a wink, then left the room.

Alexandra had an inkling as to why her mother hadn't wanted something so personal, so clearly special, to remain at their country house. During her lengthy illness, she'd often commented on how sad she would be to leave the family legacy in the hands of Harold and his wife. Mother had never cared for her son's choice of bride, believing that Rachel was more interested in the title than being part of the family. She'd proven that time and time again with her insincere actions and forceful dictations. And of course, their brother had completely changed upon his marriage. Everyone had taken note. Mother was probably worried Rachel would simply throw it all away without a second thought.

Theodora took another letter from the trunk and unfolded it. "Oh, it's another love letter from Father. It's so beautifully written." She held it to her chest. "Do you think we will ever find a love like theirs?"

"I certainly hope so," Evelina said as she went to Theodora and gave her sister a hug. "I certainly hope so."

Alexandra glanced to the clock on the mantel. "I suppose we will have to wait until tomorrow to discover what treasures awaits us."

"Couldn't we make some excuse and stay in instead?" Theodora questioned as she looked down at the dozens and dozens of letters still remaining. Alexandra would have enjoyed nothing more than staying in with her sisters, exploring the contents of the trunk together. For as long as she could remember, they'd always enjoyed looking at family treasures, especially letters. It made them feel so connected to loved ones no longer with them. They had kept their grandmother's correspondences to and from her sisters, which were always great fun to read.

"It wouldn't be polite, and besides Mr. Fuller is to be in attendance, and we need to determine if he is suitable for Miss Samuels," Alexandra said as a sense of good washed over her at the prospect of aiding a friend.

"Very well. At least we have something to look forward to if the evening is boring," Evelina added.

Several hours later, Alexandra could hardly call the Dowager Viscountess Lady Kirkwood's dinner party *boring*. With a sister seated on either side of her, along with all the other guests in the drawing room, she listened to an unfortunate scene unfold in the hallway.

"Where are you going?" Lady Kirkwood was demanding in barely hushed tones that could be heard by those seated nearest the drawing room entry.

"Out."

"We have guests and—"

"*You* have guests, Mother. I have other obligations this evening."

Alexandra could not see the exchange between mother and son happening in the corridor, but, by the sound of it, neither was pleased with the other.

"And by obligations, are you referring to your mistress?" The pain in Lady Kirkwood's voice echoed into the drawing room.

Those around the sisters stilled and waited for the next words to be spoken. Thankfully, Lord Kirkwood saved his mother from further distress by ceasing the argument and storming down the corridor, the stomp of his shoes on the marble creating a firm cadence.

Moments later, as if nothing untoward had occurred just feet away, Lady Kirkwood reentered the room. Although she smiled politely, embarrassment lined her features.

Much to the credit of everyone present, no one commented on what had just taken place or the recent absence of their hostess. Soon more guests arrived, unfortunately including some confirmed gossips like Lady Jerome and her daughter, but also Niall and some other friends.

"Oh look," Alexandra said as she motioned toward the door. "Martha is a guest this evening. I must go and greet her."

She'd last seen her dear friend two years ago in the country, when Martha was visiting her grandparents who lived nearby. It was just before Martha's first Season, and her parents had been determined their eldest of five daughters would be married by its end. Alexandra had always suspected that Martha was nervous about her prospects. She was rather tall for a woman and often complained that she looked more like a lad, but when Mr. Hadfield offered for her, it seemed her insecurities vanished, or at least that was what Alexandra had gathered from her friend's letters.

"It is so pleasant to see you after all this time, Martha," Alexandra embraced her friend as she entered the drawing room. "You look wonderful!"

"It has been far too long," Martha said with her usual sweet smile.

"Married life certainly agrees with you."

"Thank . . ." A soft shuddered cry escaped her lips as she turned away from the other guests.

"Oh my, whatever is the matter?" Alexandra whispered as she rubbed a gentle hand on her friend's back. She had never seen Martha so distraught—nor so quickly. She surveyed her options for retreat and settled on the small terrace, then guided her friend away from gossiping tongues.

Once away from the other guests, Martha began to divulge her woes. "I can't keep it in any longer! Married life is . . . horrible. I had no idea what . . ." Her words died off, leaving Alexandra wondering whatever had happened.

She took Martha's hands within her own and tried to coax her friend to speak. "Perhaps if you tell me what's the matter, I can help."

"And how are you supposed to help when you're not married and do not understand the ways of the bedroom?" Martha cried. "It's not at all pleasant and . . ." Her words died as she buried her face into her hands.

"Whatever is the matter?" Evelina said as she rushed onto the terrace, with their youngest sister on her heels.

"We saw you rush from the room," Theodora added with

concern.

Alexandra looked to her sisters and shrugged her shoulders. She didn't understand what had brought on such a state of hysterics in Martha. "So, the problem at hand is your husband? Has he mistreated you?" She felt her anger rising at the thought of anyone mistreating Martha.

They stared at Martha waiting for her to explain.

Martha shook her head. "It does concern Mr. Hadfield, but he has not misused me. I think . . . I think he doesn't find me . . ." She nodded her head this way and that. ". . . Interesting enough," she whispered. Even the dim light could not hide the fierce shade of red staining her cheeks.

Alexandra leaned in and, keeping her voice low, questioned, "What do you mean, *interesting enough?*"

Martha let out a loud huff, then even more dramatically exclaimed, "He rarely comes to my bed. I may be quite naïve, but I do understand that men like . . ." She pressed her lips together as she bobbed her head, clearly waiting for Alexandra to comprehend her meaning.

Finally realizing what Martha meant, Theodora began to say rather loudly, "Oh, do you mean, sexual inter—"

"Don't say it out loud!" The look on Martha's face was one of utter humiliation. "We should not . . . I should not have said anything. You mustn't say anything to anyone." And with that, their friend scurried back into the drawing room.

And therein lay the problem. It was a forbidden topic, even amongst friends. How were women supposed to learn and navigate through such a subject if they could not discuss matters? Not openly with strangers, of course, but it should be something that could be talked of amongst the closest of acquaintances. Alexandra and her sisters were certainly not prepared for the intimacies of married life, and up until this point, she had not contemplated them. She'd just assumed men and women married, set up a house, and the rest fell into place. But what was *the rest?*

"What was all that—" Theodora started on a whisper.

"Not here," Alexandra halted the question as they rejoined the others. Numerous eyes were on them and the last thing they needed was to draw extra attention to Martha or stir any more trouble for themselves so soon after the incident with Miss Newman.

Theodora and Evelina went to join their great-aunt, while Alexandra kept near to the terrace entrance. Her mind was reeling with all sorts of questions about what her friend had and had not disclosed. She felt for Martha. Unhappy marriages were not uncommon, but who was to blame? What was the key to a happy union?

"Is anything the matter?" Niall's concerned voice brought her back to the strange evening she was currently experiencing.

A deep sigh reverberated through her body. "No. Just pondering the complexities of humans."

The spot between Niall's brows crinkled with confusion. He pushed the spectacles further up his nose. "The complexities of humans? It sounds like a rather interesting topic," he teased.

"More vexing than interesting."

"How so?" he prompted.

How could she answer when she still hadn't formulated all her questions or found any answers? Perhaps Niall could come to her aid? A deep longing pressed against her chest, and she yearned for those carefree days with him when they had taken long walks and talked for hours about whatever crossed their minds. Before she could respond, dinner was announced.

"I suppose we will have to continue this stimulating discussion later." Niall winked then joined his mother and sister as the other guests gathered for the procession into the dining hall.

Parading into the dining hall had always struck Alexandra as unnecessary, but she supposed it did keep guests in a neat and tidy formation. She was pleased to be paired with Mr. Fuller. It would give her the perfect opportunity to discover his character and interests. On the surface, he was handsome with a pleasant, calm countenance. His two front teeth were slightly crooked, but his smile most sincere. Yes, she suspected he would do nicely for Miss Samuels.

As they entered the grand dining hall, she was impressed by the sheer size and layout of the elegant table. The *dormant du milieu* at the center of the table was most striking with its overflowing cornucopia of fruits and flowers arranged in such a way that it looked like a still life painting which belonged in a gallery.

Once seated, the conversation with Mr. Fuller flowed most naturally. He was a very pleasant fellow indeed. Her instincts were confirmed.

"My aunt informed me that you are quite proficient at the violin."

The gentleman's warm brown eyes lit up with the mention of the instrument. "Playing the violin is a passion of mine. I recently acquired one made by Jacob Stainer. He was one of most sought-after luthiers of his time. Even Mozart had one of his violins." He smiled brightly, then offered, "I apologize, Miss Grace, I am rambling. I could speak all day of music."

"That's quite all right. I know a young lady of the same persuasion."

"Really?" Interest laced the single word as he offered her ragout of celery, the spicy scent of cloves tickling her nose as he placed a serving on her plate.

"Miss Samuels is accomplished on the harp and has one of the most beautiful singing voices I've ever heard." With each word of praise she spoke, his eyes widened with interest. She was very pleased with the turn of events. With nonchalance she added, "Miss Samuels will be joining my sisters and me at Lady Turner's garden party."

The seed was planted.

Alexandra felt Evelina's gaze from across the table. She met her sister's gaze, which pleaded for assistance. Clearly, she was not enjoying the company of the gentleman beside her. She'd never met Mr. Robertson, but she had a feeling she was going to learn much about him from Evelina.

After the meal concluded, the ladies adjourned to the drawing room while most of the men stayed to consume their brandies. Alexandra noted that Niall, Mr. Fuller, and a couple of other gentlemen departed the company of the rowdier men. She wondered where they were off to and what they would discuss. Knowing Niall, it would center on the new landscaping designs he had been working on. She inwardly chuckled. Niall was certainly passionate about creating a beautiful outlook. Quite often, he would share his thoughts and ideas, all of which she found most stimulating.

Alexandra and Theodora followed the herd of feathered plumes while a still very agitated Evelina excused herself to the ladies retiring room. Alexandra was certain to get an earful later in the evening. Even Martha had departed early, complaining of a megrim, but Alexandra suspected her friend was still out of sorts after what had happened earlier in the evening.

With the men preoccupied, unintellectual conversation surrounding mundane topics was the order of the evening. It seemed that women of the *ton* could only converse about the weather, the latest fashions, and entertainments. The sisters learned that most of the ladies present were of the opinion that the newest *on dits* were the most fascinating diversions this Season.

And as if to make their point, some of the older grande dames, led by the Dowager Duchess of Blackburn and Lady Jerome, seemed intrigued by what had happened with Martha on the terrace. Clearly her tears had not gone unnoticed. It appeared that no one was safe. Oh, how Alexandra detested these rumor-mongers!

At the very least, she and her sisters were not mentioned. Now all they had to do was survive the rest of the evening.

Chapter Four

ALTHOUGH THEY EMERGED from Lady Kirkwood's dinner party untouched by the tittle-tattle that had been circulating around the room, the carriage ride back to their aunt's home was silent. Alexandra suspected Evelina was bursting with information—or more likely a fuming rant. Only when they had reached the sanctity of their private rooms did her middle sister finally speak.

"Mr. Robertson has to be without a doubt the most disagreeable man there ever was!" Evelina said as she stormed into the room and closed the door behind her.

"What—" Theodora only got one word out before Evelina interrupted her.

"I will tell you what happened," Evelina said with an exasperated wave of her arms. "Mr. Robertson could talk of nothing but himself. Throughout the entire meal, everything was about his accomplishments, his estate, his mother, his interests." She let out a loud harumph. "He is not interesting in the least, and his accomplishments are quite paltry, consisting of his ability to read an entire book, even though he has no interest in reading, and his ability to take long walks."

"He sounds like an utter—"

Evelina whipped around, fury rumbling in her voice. "And do

you know what the worst part was?"

"He does not care for poetry?" Alexandra quipped, trying to lighten the mood.

Evelina narrowed her eyes, clearly not amused. "That's not the worst part, but you may add it to the list," she said as she put her hands to her hips. "He believes women to be inferior in *all* aspects of life. He even said that men read better than women. And this coming from a man who prides himself on being able to read one book. One book!"

Not wanting her sister to wake the entire household with her tirade, Alexandra attempted to reign in Evelina's temper. In a calm voice she asked, "Is that why you disappeared after dinner?"

"I needed a moment to regain my senses, but instead of finding relief, I became more agitated."

"Mr. Robertson again?"

"Yes. No. All of them. All of the men who think so little of women." She shook her head and let out a long sigh. "I was walking to rejoin the ladies after using the necessary when I heard the men guffawing in the dining hall. I was curious about what could be so amusing so I edged up to the door and overheard one say that wives are boring in bed. And then another said that wives are meant to be obedient and that's why mistresses exist."

"All men can't possibly believe that?" Theodora questioned.

"Lord Kirkwood certainly seems to share that opinion. He went off to his mistress instead of attending his mother's dinner party, as we all heard. The men in the dining hall applauded his actions and praised his choice of consort."

But not all the men. Niall had been part of the after-dinner gaggle. She suspected, no, she *knew* he was different than other men. But why?

"We need to discover the truth," she said.

An idea jolted her senses. Could they possibly do it? It was a scandalous idea but one she would enjoy seeing to fruition. It would be to the benefit of all their friends, after all.

She was still feeling ruffled after what Martha had revealed.

She didn't know what her own future held, but one thing was for certain: she would not end up miserable like her friend.

"I know you're scheming," Evelina stated as she took a seat beside the fire, then stretched out her hands to warm them.

"I've been thinking."

"Oh dear, that can be dangerous," Theodora teased.

Laughter rumbled from within. "Precisely." The three sisters were always—according to the gossipmongers in the country—thinking too much, reading too much, and voicing their opinions far too much.

"Are you going to share your thoughts, or do we have to wrestle them from you?"

"I was thinking that we need to host a salon."

"Isn't that what we did? Friends came, we discussed the weather and the latest *on dits*. There was nothing practical, realistic, or even useful about the gathering. Really, I don't know if I can tolerate more occasions such as that," Evelina sighed.

"This would be different."

Both of her sisters turned an inquisitive gaze her way, but it was Theodora who spoke first. "How so?"

"We need to delve into forbidden topics." Alexandra paced the room, mumbling through her thoughts until the words formed into cohesive sentences. "It would be a salon for helping us all master the complexities of the male mind. How else are we not to fall victim to loveless marriages simply acquired for advancement within Society and begetting heirs?"

"I don't believe all marriages are so dispassionate," Evelina started. "Look at our parents."

"Look at Harold and his wife." Theodora let out a long sigh as she shook her head. "I am not willing to take that chance. Rachel was agreeable before they married, and once she got what she wanted, she showed her true colors, and has made life miserable for our brother."

"But how are we to discover the information we seek?" Theodora questioned, then before Alexandra or Evelina could answer, she quickly added, "And what exactly *are* we looking for?"

"We need more information before we begin. It's not just enough to watch the men at social gatherings. And what about all the places men retreat to where women have no access?" Perhaps Niall could shed some light on the subject. He wasn't the typical rake about Town—*no, he wasn't*—but he would certainly know enough to answer questions. She would have to ponder this more.

"Like taking their brandy after dinner," Evelina said with annoyance. "Or running off to their clubs and the devil knows where else."

"Perhaps we could enlist the aid of servants," Theodora suggested, interrupting their middle sister.

Evelina shook her head. "That would only work if we hosted a gathering here." She paused for a moment, then with exclaimed with great exuberance, "I've got it! At the next dinner party, when the men retire, I will sneak away and discover what they talk about. I wasn't even trying to eavesdrop at Lady Kirkwood's and look at the information I gleaned just by passing the dining hall. Just think of what I could discover if I were trying to listen."

"And how do you intend to do that?" Alexandra questioned.

"I don't know yet, but I will think of something."

"Perhaps there are more letters in the trunk that can shed light on the topic," Alexandra suggested. She went to it and lifted the lid. Hopefully somewhere within the oak cocoon, they could find answers, ease their concern, and create a plan of action. She pulled out several stacks of neatly folded letters, then turned and handed a pile to each sister. "Let's get to work."

Not caring for propriety, the girls sat on the floor in front of the warm fire, just as they had done when they were little. Before long, they were sharing the contents of the letters in their particular stack.

"Mother wrote this one when she was pregnant with Harold and Papa was in London." Evelina ran a gentle hand over the page. "She tells Papa about feeling the baby kick for the first time." She handed the letter to Alexandra. "Oh, she was so excited."

Alexandra longed for a friendship, a love, and a life—minus the illnesses—like her parents had. Would she ever find someone to share and experience these kinds of joys with?

"Oh my!" Theodora loudly exclaimed, startling Alexandra out of her musings. "This is not a sweet love letter. This is . . ."

Alexandra and Evelina turned their gaze to their youngest sister. "What?" they asked in unison.

"I had no idea . . ." Her words trailed away, and Evelina took the letter from Theodora's hand, then scanned the sheaf as Alexandra edged closer and attempted to read it over her shoulder. Heat instantly filled her cheeks.

"A man would actually do *that* to a woman?" Evelina questioned in a breathy whisper.

"Even worse! Father wanted to do *that* to Mother!" Theodora exclaimed with shock as she stood and went to the window and opened it. The cold night breeze, carrying the scent of early springtime in the city, permeated the room. Clearly Alexandra was not the only one overcome by what they were reading.

Alexandra and her sisters opened other letters from the same pile, each scanning the contents. She didn't know what they were looking for. Perhaps an explanation?

"And here's another letter. This one is from Mother to Father," Evelina said as she gently held the yellowed pages and read it to herself.

A moment later shocked green eyes met Alexandra's. "What did Mother write?" she questioned, wanting yet not wanting to know the details.

"That thing . . . in the letter from Father to Mother. Well . . ." Evelina swallowed as her cheeks reddened deeper than a ripened strawberry. "It would seem that she wanted to do the same to him."

Theodora plopped down on the sofa, shaking her head. A

moment later, Evelina joined her. Both just stared at the letter in utter disbelief.

Alexandra was at a loss for words. Only a short time ago, Martha had broken down in tears over what she'd had to endure in the marriage bed. But clearly not every woman found the *act* distasteful.

"I . . . I don't understand." She paced several feet in each direction before stopping in front of her sisters. "What makes one woman cry in despair and another want to . . . you know—"

"Perform intimacies like these?" Evelina waved her mother's letter.

"And why didn't Mother discuss such things with us?" their youngest sister said.

"We were still quite young when she first took ill. I was but sixteen," Alexandra said, emotion choking her words. "I'm sure there were so many things Mama would have wanted to say to us to guide us."

Silence filled the room weighed down by the grief they each still felt. The sisters had been so young, too young in Alexandra's estimation. Evelina had been fourteen, and Theodora not quite thirteen. It was an impressionable age for young ladies, but they had made a pact to care for their dearest mama, and for each other. Little had they realized that, one distant day, their father would slowly, painfully lose his mind. But through it all, the sisters had been together. Hot tears stung the corners of Alexandra's eyes. Soon it would all change. Soon they would marry. What then?

Evelina sniffled, then shook her head—as was her wont when trying to conceal her feelings—turning her attention to the large trunk. She lifted a wooden box from it, only this one had a carving of the mythological Three Graces on the lid. She removed the lid, revealing neatly arranged items. "There's a letter," she started, "with our names on it. And a small box for each of us." She handed the boxes to her sisters, and they each opened theirs.

"Mother gave us each a cameo with a depiction of the Three Graces," Theodora said, emotion choking her words.

Evelina then opened the letter and began to read. "My greatest desire for my girls is that you find a love and friendship like your father's and mine. Go out in the world and discover devotion and passion, and never be afraid of desire."

Theodora went to Alexandra, wrapping her arms about her. Her voice quavered as she whispered, "They truly had a beautiful life together."

"I always loved the tenderness in their eyes when they looked at each other." Evelina brushed a single finger under her eye, wiping away a tear.

Theodora then went to their middle sister, and just as she had done with Alexandra, wrapped her arms about her, resting her head on Evelina's shoulder. "I wish they were still here with us."

The words hung in the air as silence enveloped them, each lost in their own thoughts.

The sorrow that had been weighing Alexandra down magnified. She didn't want to think about those last months when their mother had been so frail and weak she could hardly move, and their father had become a shell of who he once was. She pushed those recollections to the dark recesses of her mind, desperately trying to embrace the happier times. "Do you remember when Father was teaching us to climb the oak tree near the rose garden?"

Evelina chuckled. "Mother was furious, not because of the climbing but because we were wearing dresses. She marched us straight into the house and—"

"And changed us into Harold's old breeches," Theodora ended their sister's sentence with a giggle.

"And then put on a pair herself and marched back out to the tree and climbed with us!" Laughter filled Alexandra's body. It felt good to share these memories.

"Mother was certainly a force to be reckoned with." Pride reverberated in Evelina's voice. "And Father encouraged that side of her. It was quite lovely to watch them together, especially when they believed no one was looking."

"How he adored her," Theodora said on a dreamy sigh.

"And that is what we should be striving for," Alexandra started. "Nothing less than true love and adoration." She was more determined than ever to not just settle for a marriage. She wanted passion and desire—just like her mother had encouraged in her letter. She paced again while forming her words. "We need to do exactly what Mother wanted, but first we need to understand."

"What do you suggest?" Evelina asked with curiosity.

"Perhaps there are more clues to what we should be looking for in Mama and Father's letters."

The sisters stayed up until the sun began to rise in the east, reading through the letters, reminiscing about the past, and thinking about the future. Apart from rather graphic sexual desires, it painted a wonderful picture of two people who had been in love and detested being apart, even for a day. It gave them glimpses into what could be.

◦◦◦ ❧ ◦◦◦

Chapter Five

T HE JOURNEY TO Lord and Lady Turner's estate in the countryside, just on the outskirts of Town, was most pleasant. The sky was clear with not a cloud present. Alexandra and her sisters were looking forward to the event. Not only was it a wonderful opportunity to introduce Miss Samuels to Mr. Fuller, but Evelina and Theodora were going to invite a carefully selected group of friends to their first *special* salon, *and* Alexandra would get to see Niall. Just the thought of seeing him sent a thrill through her. She knew she was just missing her dearest friend, but it felt like it had been weeks since she'd last met him, and couldn't wait to talk with him. She was desperate to get answers, and she hoped Niall could aid her in her quest for knowledge on delicate topics.

As they ascended the veranda steps, Alexandra could not help but notice the vast number of people in attendance. It appeared as if every eligible gentleman of the *ton* had turned out for the garden party. And yet, as she glanced around, all she could think about was seeing Niall.

"Miss Grace," Naomi began as she approached them, "isn't it a wonderful party? I have never seen such a spectacular array of diversions all in one place."

"Nor I, to be sure."

Lord and Lady Turner had spared no expense. There was a large music pavilion with plenty of shade for guests to enjoy the activities—lawn bowling, ring toss, cricket, and even an area reserved for an archery competition. It promised to be a very entertaining afternoon.

"My sisters and I will be hosting another salon in two days and would be pleased if you could join us. Lady Dorothy will be in attendance as well." Not that Alexandra had any intention of corrupting Niall's youngest sister, but Naomi seemed as if she was in need of an afternoon of light conversation and good company. She would just have to ensure that Naomi did not stay for the *other* salon that was to take place directly after.

"That is very kind of you to offer, but . . . but I have to decline." Naomi's lips dipped into a deep frown. "Not that I want to decline, but Mother is most particular about how I spend my time. She would never approve." The young woman ended with a shake of her head, and Alexandra's suspicions were all but confirmed; the Dowager Duchess of Blackburn did not care for Alexandra or her sisters.

"If you change your mind, the offer still stands." Her words were met with a wide smile.

"Thank you, that is most kind of you." Naomi turned her head slightly, catching her mother's figure storming toward them. "I must go." She dashed off in the opposite direction, clearly hoping to avoid the formidable dowager for at least a short time. Alexandra felt for the girl. Her whole life was being dictated by a domineering woman who only seemed to care about social standing. Thank heaven the duchess was not her own mother!

"We should probably walk in the opposite direction as well," she said to her sisters as she moved toward the rose garden. She did not want anyone to spoil the day for them. She was looking about for Niall when she spied Miss Samuels and Mr. Fuller conversing near the music pavilion. She stopped short and grabbed Evelina's hand. "Look." She nodded her head in the direction of the couple. "It would seem that Fate has stepped in."

"They're so sweet together," Theodora said.

The sisters watched with interest. Alexandra's first instinct had been correct. They made a lovely pair. It was quite obvious, even from this distance, that they'd formed an instant attachment.

"I think our skills were put to good use," Alexandra said with pride. It felt good to aid friends.

"Who shall we choose next?" Theodora questioned with excitement as she scanned the guests.

"Matchmaking is not our priority," Evelina reminded her. "We're to discover how the male mind works, invite ladies to join our salon, and share the knowledge."

"Precisely," Alexandra agreed.

Satisfied with their efforts, they each set about their task for the day. Alexandra knew just where she needed to begin. Now all she had to do was find the man in question.

"I WAS HOPING to see you today," Alexandra said as she strolled to where Niall was standing under a large and impressive oak tree. She was the epitome of beauty and confidence. The flowing silk of her lavender pelisse accentuated her soft auburn hair and deep blue eyes. Niall found himself completely lost in the sight of her. But at her words, alarm bells rose. "I need some advice and don't know where to turn."

What sort of trouble had she landed herself in? He'd been watching the sisters from a distance and had not seen or heard anything that was out of place.

A moment later, she blurted out her question. "Is there some book of etiquette that men read about how to treat a lady?"

"A book about how to treat a lady?" He was utterly confused. "Good manners are drilled into—"

"I'm not referring to manners. I'm talking about something

else entirely." Her cheeks pinkened as she worried her delectable bottom lip. Although there were guests nearby and none were within earshot, she lowered her voice. "It's a difficult topic." Once again, he wondered what sort of trouble she had discovered. Then he caught a whiff of her intoxicating fragrance that could only be described as pure Alexandra, and he knew without a doubt, he was the one in trouble. "That is to say, it seems that what a man wants in a wife is different to what he desires in a mistress."

He was completely taken off guard and responded a little too loudly, "How do you know about such things?"

"Shh," she hissed and glanced around before continuing, "Men are quite free with their tongues when—"

"Where have you been?" He wouldn't put it past Alexandra to sneak off to forbidden places in her pursuit of knowledge.

"I haven't done anything untoward." He could practically hear the unspoken word—*yet*. "Really, Niall, are you going to help or not?" She wasn't quite begging, but he knew that tone. If he didn't assist her, she would attempt something on her own.

He sucked in a deep breath. Though they could only be friends, he could, at the very least, still protect her and ensure her a happy future. "What is your question?"

"Thank you," she said with a smile and bow of her head. She didn't give him a moment to recover before plunging in. "At Lady Kirkwood's dinner party, Evelina overheard some of the men say that a gentleman would not dream of doing the things he does to his mistress with his wife. Men want an obedient wife, which clearly I will never be. So that begs the question, can a wife be a mistress?"

Confusion played in his mind. *How did she . . . where did . . . ?* Perhaps he misunderstood? "If a woman is a wife, then she could never be a mistress, unless she is unfaithful and—"

Although a fierce blush stained her cheeks, Alexandra clearly was not going to give up until she got the answers she sought. She put her hands to her hips and huffed in clear frustration. "For someone who is so intelligent, you're not very astute. I want to know if a lady can learn to be the type of woman a man would want to marry *and* desire so that he doesn't want to take a mistress. Or do men just boast and put on airs to secure the marriage and find pleasure elsewhere regardless? I want to understand what makes men the way they are."

Niall realized he was in a situation that would be very hard to get out of. They should not be discussing such things at a garden party. They should not be discussing such things at all. What was he supposed to say?

"We should not be—"

"Then I will get my answers elsewhere," she said as she started to turn.

"No." He reached out and grabbed her arm, pulling her closer. Vanilla and lavender infiltrated him, disrupting his senses. He swallowed hard, forcing down the desire he always felt for this woman. "You will not get your answers elsewhere," he growled, feeling entirely too possessive. He looked into her deep blue eyes, feeling himself sink further and further into their bewitching depths.

"So, you will help me?" she whispered as her chest rose and fell, her breath teasing his desires.

He shouldn't be holding her arm. He shouldn't be standing so close. He shouldn't be fantasizing about kissing those delectable lips or running his tongue down the column of her neck. He shouldn't . . .

"I'll make you a bargain," she said when he didn't answer, her words bringing him out of his improper thoughts.

He released her arm and took a step back, attempting to regain control. "What sort of bargain?"

"If I beat you at archery—one shot each—will you answer all my questions?"

Niall did not think he could answer *all* her questions *and* maintain his composure as a gentleman. *She could only ever be a friend*, he reminded himself.

"*If* you win, then I will answer two questions." She opened her mouth as if to reply, but he needed to ensure she would not do anything foolish, impulsive, or improper. "*And* you will not search for the remainder elsewhere."

She eyed him for long moment then held out her hand to shake. "You have an agreement."

She'd acquiesced far too easily. Alexandra was up to something.

A SHORT TIME later, their archery competition was underway. Alexandra picked up the bow and arrow from the table and went to her designated spot. Niall did the same. They glanced at one another and determination shot through her veins. He bowed his head, accepting the challenge. If she won, she would discover the answers to her questions—well, two questions at least. Why was Niall being so obstinate about her request? They'd always been able to discuss all sorts of topics and he'd never denied her inquisitiveness before. *But those had not been subjects of a forbidden nature.*

She shook off those thoughts and took her stance. She needed to focus on the task at hand. She relaxed her grip and peered down the arrow at the target. Birds chirping, hushed whispers, the rustling of leaves in the wind all faded as her concentration sharpened. She took in a slight breath and released. The arrow soared through the air with efficiency, landing just shy of the bullseye.

Cheers rippled through the audience, followed by her sisters' praise. She turned to Niall. "It is your turn, Your Grace." She knew she was being a little smug, but she didn't care. It had been an excellent shot.

Niall pushed his spectacles further up his nose then got into position. His navy-blue coat stretched across his taut back as he adjusted his stance. His gaze was centered, determined. Alexandra watched his every move, his firm hand as it pulled the string and arrow back, the muscle in his jaw tightening as he concentrated. She'd never watched him so closely, so intently. Something stirred deep within, warming her. *It must be the thrill of the competition.*

She held her breath as he released the arrow and watched it travel toward the target then strike it. She blinked several times. From this distance, it looked as if their arrows were intertwined.

He glanced at her, just as she turned to look at him. With no words spoken, they both rushed to the target.

Murmurs rose all around, getting louder as they neared the haystack.

"Who won?" someone shouted from behind.

"It looks too close to call," another answered.

Alexandra stared at it, hardly believing her eyes. Niall's arrow had landed directly next to hers, not even a hair's width apart, and infinitesimally farther from the target.

She turned to him, about to call for another pair of arrows, when he whispered, "Two questions." Then he addressed those who had gathered waiting for the outcome, stating, "I acquiesce to Miss Grace." And with that, he turned on his heel and left, leaving Alexandra more than a little confused for reasons she could not even begin to comprehend.

Was he angry? Embarrassed? She inwardly sighed. Men were certainly strange creatures.

It had been an interesting and bizarre day, she reflected later as they all prepared to leave. She had won the competition with Niall, her sisters had invited several acquaintances to the next salon—while others had invited themselves—and Niall had now completely disappeared. She didn't know what to make of the latter.

"I'm exhausted," Evelina stated as she intertwined her arm with Alexandra's.

"It doesn't appear Aunt Imogene has suffered the same effects," Alexandra said as she nodded her head in the direction of their aunt, who was walking ahead of them at double their pace. It was as if she was energized by the day's event. It was quite astonishing that, at her age, she seemed to have more energy than Alexandra and her sisters combined.

"Our next gathering will be quite the hodgepodge of guests," Theodora said under her breath as the siblings walked together toward their waiting carriage. "We may have to—"

"Miss Grace!" Alexandra heard her name in a rush from behind.

"Is anything the matter, Lady Naomi?"

Naomi was flushed and clearly out of sorts, which was not unusual for her—especially since the Season had begun—but was still a cause for concern.

"No. I just wanted to tell you that I will be at the next salon." And with that, the debutante dashed off.

"How do you suppose she changed her mother's mind?" Theodora questioned.

"Something tells me that Lady Naomi is going to sneak out." Alexandra was certain she would get an earful from Niall if his sister did, but she would deal with that when the time came.

THE FOLLOWING DAY, the Grace sisters hosted their open salon, followed by their private, members-only gathering. Alexandra had hardly slept a wink, too excited by the prospect of finally being able to discuss important issues, and also of being able to offer a place for friends to voice their concerns without censure.

Tea and biscuits were served at the first salon, conversation about the weather and upcoming events flowed freely, and all but a few selected guests left at the appointed time. Even Lady Naomi, much to Alexandra's relief, took her leave with the others. It would have been awkward to come up with some excuse to send her away while others remained. Now was when their true salon would begin.

"Thank you for staying, ladies. We wanted to invite you to join us for a more exclusive meeting." With Alexandra's words, the remaining ladies' ears seemed to perk up. "But before I continue, my sisters and I want to ensure that all of you will be the souls of discretion."

Without even a moment's hesitation, Lady Dorothy, Miss Ashton, and Miss Raine all said, "Of course." It was nice to have friends one could trust.

"We want to discuss—"

Miss Raine blurted her question, "Are we going to discuss men?"

"I certainly hope so!" Lady Dorothy exclaimed with a chuckle.

"Me, too! After my narrow escape from Mr. Markham last Season, I don't ever want to be taken advantage of again."

"Discussing men is certainly one of the topics," Evelina said, then posed the question, "Why are we kept in the dark about matters of marriage?"

Miss Raine responded with confidence, "Not entirely in the dark. We are taught how to host balls, be a good hostess—"

"That's not what I mean."

"You're absolutely correct," Lady Dorothy said. "Our mothers do not share the intimate details of what happens when a man and woman are alone. I asked my eldest sister about the marriage bed because my mother won't answer any of my questions. But Joan would only tell me that she keeps her clothes on and eyes closed. As if that helps!"

"My mother uses odd, made-up words anytime I query," Miss Ashton said.

"At least your mother talks to you," Miss Raine complained. "Mine just tells me it's my duty to listen to my future husband and please him. Even my brother, who is a rake, won't discuss anything besides which gentlemen is suitable and the weather. What are we to do?"

"That is exactly what we're going to try and decide upon," Evelina stated with confidence.

Alexandra knew what she and her sisters were curious about, but did others think the same as they? She wanted to make certain she was prepared when the time came to talk to Niall. "What questions do we want answered?"

Long seconds passed before the ladies started blurting out their concerns and queries in rapid succession, each issue blending into the next.

"What is the marriage bed truly like?"

"How does one kiss?"

"Why does a husband seek a mistress?"

"How does one even please a husband?"

"Do women really keep all their clothes on? Even their corsets?"

"Do all men truly look like those Corinthian males you see in paintings?" Lady Dorothy then answered her own question. "My father certainly does not. He has to turn sideways to enter a room."

Laughter rang through the room at that admission.

The sounds around Alexandra faded as the recollection of Niall's coat stretching across his back while his firm hands gripped the bow entered her mind. She suspected he was more of a Corinthian standard.

Where did that thought come from?

Heat rose up and across her cheeks. She had never thought of Niall in such a way. He certainly *was* handsome, and when his full lips smiled at her, his eyes softened and caressed her soul. *Oh no!* She shouldn't be thinking of him in such a way, despite how overwhelmingly attractive he was. He was everything she'd ever dreamt about in a husband and—

No! she commanded her mind.

Niall was promised to Nerissa, and their engagement would be announced any day now. And besides, he did not feel the same way about her. They were friends. That was all.

This conversation about kissing and physique and . . . it was clouding her thoughts. Perhaps this was why mothers were reluctant to share intimate details—for fear of corrupting their daughters' minds.

Another round of laughter echoed through the room, bringing her back to the present. Thankfully, the ladies' questions had become more amusing, and she was quickly able to regain her senses, hopefully without either of her sisters suspecting her direction of thought.

"Why aren't women allowed to race horses?"

"Or duel for the sake of their own honor?"

"And why can't women stay in the dining room, drinking brandy and smoking cigars?" Miss Raine demanded, then burst into laughter.

"Perhaps we need to try a few of these as part of an experiment," Evelina suggested with a sly smile.

"I don't know how to even pick up a sword, let alone duel," Miss Ashton said. "And if word gets out about what we are doing, it could ruin our chances of making a suitable match."

"Our actions will just have to remain clandestine," Alexandra offered.

"How do you suggest we begin?" Miss Raine questioned with eagerness.

"My sisters and I have discussed this. Perhaps there are clues in what men are saying at the various events, how they are acting, what excuses they give for being late to or not attending an event. We should all take mental notes and report our findings at the next salon."

By the time the gathering concluded, Alexandra was feeling rejuvenated. Now all she had to do was claim her prize from Niall.

⸻ ❧ ⸻

Chapter Six

NIALL SUSPECTED THE reason for his mother's illness was that she did not want to attend Lady Archibald's soirée. They'd had a falling out years ago when Lady Archibald's son refused to consider Niall's eldest sister as a wife. Not that either Nancy or Archibald had desired the match in the first place, but the duchess had taken issue just the same and vowed to never speak to Lady Archibald ever again.

Regardless of the absurdity of the excuse, he was pleased to have a night away from Mother, and he suspected his sister felt the same. Leaning up against the wall, he watched Naomi dance the quadrille with Mr. Norley. He'd had a pleasant conversation earlier about crop rotation with the fellow. Norley was quite knowledgeable and had given Niall an insight into how to address an issue on one of his estates.

Out of the corner of his eye, he spied Lady Nerissa conversing with Lady Dorothy. He supposed he *should* ask the woman he was promised to for a dance, although she'd yet to acknowledge his presence. Every time he glanced her way, her features tightened in worry, almost in fear, as if this was the moment they were to announce their engagement.

"I thought I would find you here holding up the wall." Despite Alexandra's *bon mot*, the warmth of her voice rippled through him. She looked even more lovely tonight than she had at the garden party. Panic suddenly seized him. *The questions.* He'd completely forgotten about them. Well, not really, but he'd hoped she had.

"I was wondering when I can claim my prize?"

Clearly, she had not.

"This isn't exactly the time or place to discuss such topics." He thought his excuse might buy him some time.

For the second instance in a short span, he was wrong.

"No one is near, and besides, it's not as if we can be alone." Images of being by himself with her, kissing her, flashed through his mind. *Control yourself. You're practically engaged—to a woman of your mother's choosing.*

The argument continued on in his head until Alexandra's soft prompting broke through his thoughts. "Niall?"

He blinked several times, then acquiesced. "What is your first question?"

Her face lightened. "Why does a husband seek a mistress?"

As unfortunate as the question was, it was not as intimate as he thought it might be. "I would think many men are unhappy with marriage being foisted upon them."

Her gaze turned thoughtful, almost solemn. "Will you seek a mistress after your marriage to Lady Nerissa?" Very few knew of the situation with Lady Nerissa. In a moment of weakness, he'd confided in Alexandra although only after she'd been sworn to secrecy. She'd kept his secret, and for that he was grateful.

"No, I won't." As much as he desired another, he would never dishonor the woman he'd married. His declaration seemed to please her.

"What is another reason why a man would want a mistress?"

"That's a third question, Alex."

"Not really, Your Grace," she offered with a crooked half-smile that sent his pulse racing. "It's merely a continuation of the first." Ah, so that was how she was going to get around having had her two questions answered. Still, he couldn't deny her.

"I'll let it slide this time." She raised a quizzical brow, waiting for him to respond. "Very well." He thought of all the reasons why his father had taken a mistress. The words slipped from his mouth before he could stop them. "My father believed there was less of an attachment to a mistress. That demands were not being pushed upon him, that he could enjoy what women had to offer without . . ."

This was getting too personal. Before he died, Father had lectured Niall on what was expected of him as a duke, but the speech did not end there. Papa had told him it was perfectly acceptable to take a mistress, to visit houses of ill repute, just as long as he did not abuse his wife and did not stir up *too* much gossip, since gossip was never avoidable. Niall had been twelve at the time.

On that distant day, he'd vowed not to become like his sire. Through the years, he'd held firm to that vow. He was not like his father, and he never would be. He valued himself.

Alexandra was silent. Perhaps he'd said too much. Good. Maybe she wouldn't be so inquisitive in the future.

"I have another question."

For the third time that evening, she proved him wrong. This was not going well for him. If his sister hadn't been enjoying herself so immensely, he would have called it quits and left.

He'd already said too much and knew he would regret asking, but—"What is the question?"

She worried her bottom lip with an enticing shyness, just as she had on the day of the garden party, then whispered, "How does one even please a husband?"

Oh, eternal damnation, but he was going to hell. "That is something to be explored between you and your—"

"But it isn't always the case." With each word she spoke, her voice grew louder. "Mrs. Ha . . . I mean, my friend shared information regarding her marriage, and it was—"

"Alexandra," he said her name with firmness, hoping to stop her enquiries. "The only advice I can give you is that you must do what feels natural, whatever you desire to do." And with that, he walked away, desperate for a drink.

ALEXANDRA AND HER sisters had greeted numerous guests into their aunt's home over the past few weeks at their salons, and today would be no exception. A few of the ladies invited would stay for all of the discussions, but most would leave after the main gathering. And that was just the way the sisters had planned it. They could not risk fair-weather friends—or worse, those prone to gossip—discovering the truth of what actually occurred at their private salons.

She glanced at the clock in the study. Their guests should be arriving shortly for today's salon. There was just enough time to gather the cards when Evelina came rushing into the room, her face red as a strawberry.

"Whatever is the matter?" Alexandra questioned. "I was just on my way—"

"The parlor is full of ladies," she huffed in labored breaths.

"They're a little early but that isn't cause for concern." She wasn't sure what the issue was.

Although her voice was low, her tone was firm. "They're not our usual guests."

She swallowed hard as the meaning of her sister's words took root. "Not our—"

"Miss Jerome is here," her sister uttered with disdain. "Theodora is with her now."

"Oh no." Alexandra's stomach sank. To say Miss Jerome was a gossip was an understatement. The woman simply could not discover the truth about what went on at their gatherings. They'd planned for such a situation, although she'd never suspected it would be Miss Jerome who would show up unannounced. Alexandra reassured her sister, "It will be fine. Keep the conversation to the weather, the upcoming masked ball, and . . ." Something else, but what? *Think Alexandra, think.*

"We could . . . oh, I don't know." Seeing her normally composed sister flummoxed was causing the anxiety to rise within her at a rapid pace. "One thing is for certain—I do not care for her at all. I just know she is up to something."

"Go and aid Theodora. I will make certain the tea is delivered posthaste, and that there are extra sweets for our unexpected guests." Their aunt had instructed Cook to prepare whatever the girls would like to serve and to spare no expense, which meant there was usually plenty of food for all. She hoped the unexpected additions wouldn't trouble Cook too much.

Evelina tucked some loose strands of hair back into place, smoothed her hands down the front of her dress, took in a deep breath, and left the room much more composed than when she'd first arrived.

Alexandra gathered the playing cards, steeled her nerves, and prepared for battle. With Miss Jerome in attendance, there simply was no other action appropriate.

A short time later, all the ladies had arrived, and Alexandra was speaking to Miss Ashton when she heard Theodora exclaim from across the room, "By Zeus!"

Oh dear. It must be serious if Theodora was using their codeword for trouble. She glanced in the direction of where Theodora looked and her insides instantly reacted, churning and constricting. *Lady Mavis.*

As if it were not bad enough to have the unpleasant Miss Jerome present, her crony was here as well. Not only was Lady Mavis the daughter of a duke and possessed of a massive dowry, but she was another notorious gossip. If she discovered what truly went on at the salon, it would be most devastating for their prospects.

Evelina brushed past Alexandra and whispered, "Operation Curetes." Another coded phrase for a simple game they'd devised for such an emergency. They didn't care if they were made fun of for being naïve—it was the lesser of the two evils. The two sisters strolled side by side toward Lady Mavis, Theodora joining them.

"Lady Mavis, so wonderful you could join us this fine afternoon," Alexandra greeted with exuberance. She would not give the unpleasant woman any fodder. "You remember my sisters, Miss Evelina, and Miss Theodora?"

"Yes." Lady Mavis scanned the room, looking from one guest to the next. "So, this is your little intellectual salon?" The sarcasm and disdain dripped from her words like a spring shower.

"We prefer to call it a social gathering," Evelina said in a restrained tone that was laced with irritation.

Alexandra ignored Lady Mavis's slight, pasted on a smile, and said, "We were just about to play a game. Would you care to join us?"

The duke's daughter nodded slightly, then took a seat on the sofa next to Miss Jerome. It did not come as a surprise that the two had formed a friendship and could often be found together.

Theodora grabbed a bouquet of flowers from the side table, then went to the center of the room to explain the game. "We are going to play a variation of Tinker, Tailor, Soldier, Sailor," she started. It was a childhood game and quite juvenile, but that was exactly why they had chosen it. It was meant to throw ill-intentioned ladies off the scent of what their true purpose was at the gathering.

"Does everyone know how to play?" Evelina questioned as Theodora passed out the flowers.

"Of course we do. It's what we played as children," Miss Jerome's tone was heavy with condescension.

Alexandra and her sisters ignored the commentary and continued on with the game. Soon the ladies were counting out the petals on their respective flowers. "Tinker, tailor, soldier, sailor, rich man, poor man, beggar man, thief . . ." The rhyme was repeated until all petals were counted and the ladies revealed which of those characters they would marry. Bouts of laughter resounded around the room from all except two.

"I cannot believe I've wasted an entire afternoon with this nonsense," Lady Mavis declared as she stood, Miss Jerome following suit. "I bid you good day." She then turned and stormed from the room, with Miss Jerome close behind.

Alexandra glanced to where her sisters sat and smiled. Their operation had been a success, the antagonists had left, and those who remained could enjoy the rest of the afternoon. Another pleasant half hour passed before all but a couple of ladies departed. Those who remained were trusted and intimate friends.

"It was quite lovely how you dealt with Lady Mavis," Miss Raine commented. "I wish I was in possession of such fortitude, especially when dealing with my mother and brother." With a shake of her head, she rolled her eyes then let out a long sigh.

"It doesn't come easily, and it slips from time to time, but we can teach you," Evelina stated with confidence.

"I would like to learn as well," Miss Ashton said as she worried her hands. "I don't like being talked down to by Miss Jerome. It has happened more than once."

"Never worry, we are all in this together." Theodora clasped her hands together. "Oh, I almost forgot to tell you. A note arrived from Miss Samuels as we were assembling. She's engaged to Mr. Fuller."

"That is wonderful news. I'm certain they will be happy together," Alexandra said. She was truly pleased for the couple. At least one of their friends had made a good match this Season. "Now, let's discuss our findings."

The remaining ladies talked about the men they'd observed at various social events. It seemed that they were all reporting the same thing. The men were publicly kind to the ladies, especially those with larger dowries, offered compliments, and kept to appropriate topics of conversation.

"How are we ever to understand when we cannot spend any time alone with them?" Lady Dorothy questioned.

Miss Raine naïvely presented her solution. "Perhaps we should just ask them what they desire?"

"No, we mustn't do that," Evelina stated in a practical voice. "We do not want to ruin our chances or be labeled as lightskirts."

"Lady Dorothy, did you discover anything?"

"Only that Mr. Rodney never stops talking about the size of his estate," she said then shook her head. "Through the entire dinner, that was all he discussed. It was really quite tiring."

Miss Raine giggled, then blurted out, "Do you think when a man is boasting about how large his estate is he's really boasting about the size of his . . ." She glanced downward, then raised her wiggled her brows. "You know."

"How do you know about such things?" Miss Ashton's shocked voice reverberated through the room.

"My brother is a rake, and I am prone to eavesdropping." She covered her mouth as she laughed, then moments later regained her senses. "I overheard him tell one of his friends that Mr. Robertson is lacking in the gentleman's department." She shook her head. "Only that is not what he called it to his friends. And when I asked him about it later, he reprimanded me for spying."

"And?" Lady Dorothy and Theodora questioned at the same time.

"And . . ." she drew out the single word before continuing. "He did not wish to discuss the subject further."

"That's it?" Evelina asked, disappointment lining her words.

"Yes, besides an immense scolding about how I should know my place and act like a lady instead of a country bumpkin. Yes, that was all he said. And this coming from a rake." It was clear Miss Raine did not think highly of her brother, especially at the moment.

"What are we to do?"

"It is rather unfortunate that we do not have access to where the men go." Miss Raine's not-so-innocent comment stirred an idea in Alexandra's mind. One that she dared not discuss with this circle of friends. She would wait until she was alone with her sisters.

SEVERAL HOURS LATER, the sisters were readying for the evening's entertainments. Now was as good as any time to present her idea.

"I've been thinking—"

"I knew you were up to something," Evelina said as she eyed her sister's reflection in the mirror. "Whenever you're deep in thought, your left eyebrow raises ever so slightly."

Alexandra's hand went to her brow. She didn't know what she expected to discover, but it felt the same as the right one. It was a very intimate detail to notice, one that she hadn't ever been aware of herself.

"I never noticed that," Theodora said. "I will have to pay closer attention to it in the future."

"She's been doing it for quite some time, especially when her thoughts lean to the inappropriate, I suspect. Just like at the—"

"Oh, enough about my eyebrows," Alexandra interrupted with a huff. "Do you want to know what I was thinking or not?"

"Of course we do," Evelina said as she turned and embraced Alexandra. "You know I am only having a little fun."

"I know." Her tone turned most serious, then she practically blurted out her scheme. "I was thinking I should dress as a man and go to one of their . . . you know, the places they gather."

"But you don't have access to White's or—"

"I'm not referring to White's or any place that's similar. I'm referring to other places, the ones that rakes and gamblers attend."

"What if you're caught?"

"I won't be. I will wear breeches, keep my hair pulled back under a hat, and my face down," she said with confidence. "How are we supposed to get our answers if we don't take this risk?"

"I suppose you're right," Theodora said. "But how will you discover where men go?"

"Miss Raine."

"Miss Raine?" her sisters questioned in unison.

Alexandra nodded her head. "Miss Raine mentioned that she was prone to eavesdropping *and* that her brother is a rake. She can find out where *he* goes." She clasped her hands together. "It is a perfect solution. I will ask her tonight."

Just the possibility of uncovering more sent a thrill straight through her. What would she discover? Who would be in attendance?

Just imagine all the information I could glean from such an adventure.

Chapter Seven

THREE DAYS HAD passed since Alexandra had enlisted the aid of Miss Raine. She hadn't wanted to divulge her entire scheme and so only informed the other woman that she was gathering information to see if there was a connection between all their findings. It was a partial truth. She *was* collecting information, but she wanted to keep the part about dressing up as a man a secret.

Evelina managed to procure gentlemen's attire for them from a trunk that had belonged to their brother and been forgotten at their aunt's house. It didn't matter if Alexandra was slightly out of fashion. And they had managed to alter the clothing slightly, so it wasn't too big. She was planning to be inconspicuous regardless, and she needn't worry about breaking her promise to Niall—because she hadn't promised she wouldn't wear breeches in Town, only that she knew it would be improper to be seen in them. She would simply conceal her identity and that would solve that problem.

This evening she would visit a gaming hell that Miss Raine had discovered in her eavesdropping that also hosted beautiful women, presumably the ones that men made into mistresses. The sisters agreed that, after dinner, they would slip out together, each dressed in male attire. Evelina and Theodora were to keep watch outside the building while Alexandra would sneak in and take a look around then leave unnoticed a half hour later.

"Remember the plan," Evelina said as they approached the address late that evening after being delivered around the corner from their destination by a hack. The driver, thankfully, had not been a curious sort. "Stay in the shadows, don't talk to anyone, and meet back here in thirty minutes."

"Don't tarry longer. It's rather chilly out tonight," Theodora said as she pulled Papa's coat closer about her.

"Don't worry, I won't be long."

Alexandra was just starting to leave when her youngest sister halted her. "Your hair is slipping." She stepped in and tucked Alexandra's soft curls further into the hat and pulled it down lower, securing them in place. "Now you're ready," she whispered with nervous excitement.

Alexandra sauntered off the way she'd been practicing all afternoon. It simply would not do to glide into a gaming hell when she was dressed as a man *and* wanting keep her identity a secret. Someone would be certain to notice. Perhaps she should have reconsidered. There were any number of things that could go wrong.

No, don't think about those.

She stayed to the rear of a group of rowdy young men, following in behind them. Adrenaline rushed through her veins as the first obstacle was tackled. Just as Theodora had reminded her, she kept moving, making a circuit around the room, trying to blend in with those around her and not attract any notice. Her shoulders sagged. There wasn't anything unexpected happening here. Men were gambling and drinking while attractive women enticed them.

Laughter from a far corner caught her attention. Lord Dougherty was clearly in his cups and quite oblivious to those around him. He slapped his hand on the bottom of a passing serving girl then pulled her onto his lap, whispering into her ear. A few minutes later, the woman edged away, took his hand, and led him to a dark hallway.

Alexandra was curious about where they were going. What happened down that corridor? Who else was there? Questions swirled in her head, but common sense won and she stayed in the main room, watching the rest of the crowd. She would have to pepper Niall with more questions the next time she saw him. Well, without revealing where she'd been, that was for certain.

She wished she could get closer and listen to conversations, discover why the man playing cards kept tapping the table excessively, or why the woman with the ample bosom was leaning so close to . . . oh no, Lord Redford. And he was clearly *not* in his cups.

Not only was Lord Redford quite perceptive, but she'd also danced with him at various events and had even been partnered with him for dinner at Lady Lamden's earlier in the week. He was sure to recognize her if he came close.

Stay calm.

She took in a deep breath and slowly retreated the same way she'd come in. It felt as if it was taking an hour to reach the exit instead of just a few minutes. Thankfully, her flight went unnoticed, and she slipped outside without being detected.

Her sisters were waiting in a darkened area just beyond the house. Neither of them spoke as she rejoined them, and then they hurriedly caught another hack to take them back home. Only once they were in their rooms did Alexandra divulge what she'd seen.

"There was nothing shocking, nothing out of the ordinary. Men were drinking too much, gambling too much, and talking loudly. Except for Lord Dougherty disappearing down a dark corridor with a woman, it all seemed like any other event, just rowdier."

"Did you happen to discover what was down the corridor?" Theodora asked.

"No. I didn't want to chance being discovered." Although the evening had not been successful, she would not give up. There had to be other ways to glean information and aid their cause.

"Perhaps that is where our answers lie." Evelina stated, clearly not satisfied with the outcome of tonight's experiment either.

"Down a dark corridor?"

"No, yes, only part." Alexandra then clarified, "Behind closed doors."

And I know just who to ask.

THE NEXT MORNING brought with it ample sunshine and the opportunity to take a stroll at Vauxhall Gardens. Aunt Imogene had a prior engagement, but was insistent that the sisters enjoy the fine day, just as long as they took a maid with them.

Almost as soon as they arrived, Alexandra was pleased to spy Niall with his sister strolling along the Grand Walk. And, importantly, they were without the dowager duchess. She turned and whispered to her sisters, "Distract Naomi while I speak with Niall."

Evelina and Theodora gave each other a peculiar look, which she would have to ask them about later. First, she needed a moment alone with Niall so she could ask another question.

"Good morning, Your Grace, Lady Naomi," Theodora called out with more exuberance than truly necessary.

Naomi rushed to their side, instantly engaging in conversation with her sister. Now was Alexandra's opportunity to speak with Niall.

"I was hoping to see you today." Niall smiled warmly with her words. She'd never noticed what a lovely smile he had. *Stop that!*

"Why do I get the impression you want something?"

"Can't a friend comment on wanting to see another friend, Your Grace?"

"They most certainly can, *Alex*. But my suspicion still stands."

She was enjoying the playful banter. Whenever Niall was

near, she felt more relaxed, as if she could be herself. That was quickly becoming a rarity and was the reason why getting answers was so important. She didn't want to lose who she was or what she enjoyed when she finally found a husband. She wanted what she had with Niall, only more.

"All right, you win. I do have another question." She didn't know if he would agree to answer another query, but it was worth a try.

He let out a long sigh and looked heavenward. A moment later, much to her surprise, he met her gaze. "What is it?"

She wasted no time in asking. "What happens behind closed doors? Between a man and woman at, let's say . . . a club or gaming hell, for example?"

His eyes narrowed, searching hers. "Please tell me you haven't done anything reckless."

Alexandra glanced to where her sisters were still conversing with Naomi. She lowered her voice, "My reputation is fully intact if that is what is concerning you."

"You are incorrigible."

"I will take that as a compliment," she said with a wide smile. "Now will you answer my question?"

He shook his head, clearly contemplating what to do. When he finally spoke, his voice was low. She strained to hear his response. "The men who engage in activities at those places are not looking for meaningful relationships. They are seeking pleasure, pure and simple."

She swallowed hard, wanting to know *exactly* what he meant by pleasure. Her parents had clearly shared passion. Heat crept up her body as improper thoughts flooded her mind and more questions formed on her lips. "But what—"

"Alexandra, you need to stop this before your reputation suffers or worse." His stance brooked no argument. "You should be concentrating on enjoying the Season, finding a husband. This *cannot* continue."

She assumed *this* meant their recent conversations. Is that what Niall truly expected her to do? To just find a husband, move away from him, to never see each other except in Town? Would they no longer be friends? Her heart constricted with the thought that their friendship might be over, that his life, his heart, would belong to another, that he would share those intimacies with Lady Nerissa.

She could not shake the image of Niall and Lady Nerissa together, embracing, touching. Her stomach burned as pain shot up her chest. She needed to get away, to find quiet solitude. She sucked in a deep breath to steady her nerves.

"Thank you for your assistance, Your Grace. I will not bother you any further." She rushed from his side to rejoin her sisters. She needed to leave *now*. "I should like to return home."

She didn't have to look at either Evelina or Theodora to know that they were staring at her with gaping mouths. She would not discuss her feelings, especially because at this moment they weren't clear to her. What had just happened? She'd never been at odds with Niall before, never felt the need to flee from him.

What had started out as a lovely day had quickly soured.

Days had passed and still Alexandra had not discovered all the answers she needed. Worse, she had not seen Niall at any of the functions she'd attended since they'd met at Vauxhall. Why couldn't she stop thinking about him and their last meeting? She couldn't very well march up to his door and demand he speak with her. She couldn't even send a note without raising suspicion. What was wrong with her? She was upset and didn't know what to do about it.

Her great-aunt's solution to Alexandra's low spirits was to attend a ball hosted by the elusive Lord Grimsby. Perhaps that was exactly what she needed, a frivolous evening of entertainment to distract her mind from Niall, her dilemma, and her questions.

The evening would serve more than one purpose. Alexandra and her sisters had decided to play matchmaker again. They had each noticed that Naomi seemed to have formed an attachment to Mr. Norley at Lady Turner's garden party. He was a very pleasant gentleman, although he wasn't titled. Such things didn't bother them, but Alexandra suspected that the Dowager Duchess of Blackburn would not share their sentiments.

Tonight, they were to set at least one of their plans into motion.

The crush was quite intense, delaying their arrival. By the time they entered the grand ballroom, the dancing was well underway, the card room was overflowing with excited guests, and the refreshment hall was full of gossiping mamas.

No sooner had they entered the ballroom than Mr. Norley approached. He cut a fine figure in beige breeches and a dark brown coat. From what the sisters had learned, not only was Mr. Norley's family highly regarded but he received four thousand pounds a year and had a lovely estate near Bath.

"May I have the pleasure of the next dance, Miss Theodora?" Mr. Norley asked then offered a simple bow.

"I would be most pleased, Mr. Norley." As they strolled away, Alexandra heard her youngest sister inquire, "Are you familiar with Lady Naomi?" She inwardly laughed. Her sister had gone straight to the task at hand. She suspected that if it were up to Theodora, she would have the pair announcing their engagement tonight and the banns published tomorrow.

She watched as both her sisters engaged in the lively dance. She was pleased they were enjoying themselves. This was how it ought to be, especially after so much heartache. It was what their parents would have wanted. If only she could escape her feelings and just enjoy the moment, too.

Once the dance ended, Mr. Norley returned Theodora to their party, while Evelina was engaged for the next dance by Mr.

Greenford. The sisters had heard rumors that he was in need of funds. If anyone could uncover further information, it would be Evelina.

With Theodora deep in conversation with Aunt Imogene, Alexandra took the opportunity to take in her surroundings. This ballroom wasn't like any other she'd been in previously. The walls were paneled in mahogany with elegantly elaborate wall sconces placed every few feet. The grand chandelier overhead sparkled against the dark paneled ceiling. Oddly, however, the room lacked flowers adorning the vast space or any other feminine adornment. This was clearly a man's house. And she couldn't help but notice that the room lacked mirrors to reflect the candlelight. Tittle-tattle had circulated about Town regarding Lord Grimsby, but she'd yet to be introduced to him. She wondered if any of it was true?

"Who is that?" Theodora questioned as she elbowed Alexandra in an attempt to get her attention. "Over there, in the shadows?"

Alexandra glanced over to where a tall, lone, masked figure stood in the darkest corner of the ballroom, where no candles had been lit. She opened her mouth to state that she didn't know, when Aunt Imogene explained. "That is Lord Grimsby, the Earl of Grimsby." She tsked several times before continuing. "Such a tragic story."

Theodora pulled her gaze from the earl and glanced at their great-aunt. "What happened?" she whispered with curiosity. Trust her youngest sister to be sympathetic to a distressing tale. Ever since their parents' illnesses, it had been thus.

Aunt Imogene leaned in and told them in an undertone, "Nearly twelve years ago, there was a terrible fire at Grimsby Hall. Lord Grimsby rescued his mother and younger sister and a servant from the blaze, but when he tried to rescue his brother and father, he was injured by falling debris. That is why he wears a mask, keeps to the shadows, and avoids society. Some call him the Phantom of Grimsby Hall."

"What is he doing in London *and* hosting a ball if he wants to avoid society?" Alexandra wanted to know more but settled on the most obvious question.

"To find a suitable match for his cousin and heir, Mr. Eastwick. Lord Grimsby has vowed to never marry but wants to ensure the earldom is secure." Aunt Imogene eyed the sisters. "Perhaps one of you would suit Mr. Eastwick. He is quite handsome, and with what he stands to inherit—"

"I have no intention of marrying just because a gentleman is handsome or wealthy," Theodora argued then put a hand to her chest. "What matters most is what's on the inside, in his heart. Is he a good man? A caring man?"

Just then, Mr. Greenford ushered Evelina back to their little party. His body was rigid, his mouth pursed tight, and his eyes narrow and full of annoyance. He made a formal bow, then left without a word.

"What happened on the dance floor?"

"Mr. Greenford was far too interested in boasting about the size of his estate and how much he spent on renovations, rather than in a simple conversation about poetry. He couldn't even name a poet, let alone recite a poem! And, what is it with men boasting about the size of their estates?" She crossed her arms. "Also I think I insulted his intelligence."

"Why do you say that?"

"Because he murmured under his breath that no dowry was worth enduring such an interrogation. He is without a doubt the dullest man I have ever encountered."

The Season was progressing at a rapid pace and none of the sisters were even remotely close to making a match; not one gentleman had caught their eye. The marriage mart was becoming a dull, never-ending game of trying to discover a gentleman's true character, and the last thing Alexandra wanted was for her—or her sisters—to fall victim to a fortune hunter or endure a loveless, passionless marriage.

Worse still was her trouble with Niall. She longed for the

friendship and easy, carefree conversations they'd shared when they were in the country. In Town, there were too many restrictions, too many unknowns. And she was becoming consumed by her quest for knowledge of the opposite sex, which she knew vexed him. Yet, no matter how hard she and her sisters tried, they could not acquire the answers they sought, with or without his help.

Across the room, she noticed Niall, standing as usual against a column. He was so different at these events, so uncomfortable. Guilt streaked through her. She should go and apologize for her earlier behavior. It had been unfair to put him in the position of having to explain things that ought to be reserved for a mother.

She was just about to make her way to him when Miss Raine brushed past her side, handing her a note. Now was definitely not the time or place to read it, so she tucked it away in her reticule. Hopefully, it contained information that they wanted.

NIALL'S PULSE QUICKENED as he spotted Alexandra coming his way. It had been days—but felt like months—since they had last spoken. He regretted his firm tone, but he could not have *those* sorts of conversations with her.

It was killing him being this close to her, and yet, there was nothing he could do, nothing he could say—well, at least not the words he wanted to declare. Being promised to Lady Nerissa since he was a lad had never bothered him more. He realized now just how much he'd come to care for and desire Alexandra.

Truth be told, he'd never thought about a love match for himself. His parents had not had one, and his two married sisters had not done so for love, both too consumed with title and status to worry over it. They seemed content enough, but Niall didn't want simply content. He wanted passion and desire. He wanted Alexandra.

"May I have a word with you?" Alexandra asked. Then she quickly added, "Don't worry, no more questions." She offered a small, lopsided smile.

He desperately wanted to talk to her too. He offered his arm, and they walked in the direction of the veranda. Numerous couples had gathered there, viewing the illuminated gardens below. He chose a secluded corner with the hope that their conversation would not be overheard. With all the chatter swirling around them, it would be rather difficult for eavesdroppers, but he was not going to take the chance regardless.

"I wanted to—," she started, just as he said, "I want to apologize."

"You have nothing to apologize for, Niall," she said with sincerity. "I should have never asked those things of you."

"And I should not have been angry with you." He pushed his spectacles further up his nose, inhaling deeply. "I was trying to maintain the utmost decorum, and in the process I hurt you."

"Do you never want to throw decorum to the wind and just do what you desire?"

He struggled with his words. At that moment, all he wanted to do was toss duty over the balustrade, pull her into his embrace, and kiss her. It was a nice fantasy but he could never allow it to happen.

"What I desire is never a possibility. Duty seems to always reign superior in my world."

She stared at him intently for long seconds before turning her gaze to the gardens beyond. On a breathy whisper, she said, "It's a lovely night."

Words disappeared from his mind. He'd been friends with her practically their whole lives and had never had an issue talking with her until now. What was he supposed to say?

Agree with her, you dolt.

She shifted her gaze, her lovely blue eyes meeting his. They sparkled like stars in the clear night sky. "You're awfully silent. What are you thinking about?"

How was it possible that he could not form two coherent words? Heat radiated between them. Did she feel it too?

Finally, he found a word. "You." Of course, it was not the word he should have spoken.

She didn't break the gaze but stared at him as if she were only just truly seeing him.

Quickly clearing his throat, he spoke the first reasonable lie he could think of. "Your marriage prospects, of course. Has any gentleman caught your eye this Season?"

"No. And I truly do not care for being in Town. I miss the countryside and the long walks, and reading by the fire, and . . ."

"The peace."

"And friendship." She held his gaze.

"You will always have it."

"Thank you, Your Grace," she said with sincerity.

"Alex, I—"

"Niall," Theodora said as she rushed onto the veranda. "Your mother is looking for you. Naomi is crying and creating quite a scene."

"Duty calls."

Would it ever cease to call, to dictate, to infiltrate every aspect of his life until all that was left was . . . duty?

DUTY.

Alexandra was coming to detest that single word. It was tearing her dearest friend away from her, creating a distance that was breaking her heart. Oh, why did things have to change?

Niall rushed back into the ballroom, leaving Alexandra and Theodora alone. She pushed her worries to the back of her mind and focused on the current issue. "What is the matter with Naomi?"

"The dowager duchess caught her sipping lemonade."

"Of all the scandalous acts," Alexandra chuckled.

"With Mr. Norley!" Theodora lowered her voice to a mere whisper. "She was quite vocal about the gentleman's lack of title and how no daughter of a duke would ever associate with such riffraff."

"She is quite frightening in her opinions."

"That is an understatement." Theodora shook her head and took in a deep breath, then turned her attention to Alexandra. "And what was going on between you and Niall just now?"

"Just an apology."

Theodora raised a quizzical brow. "An apology?" she questioned as if not believing the explanation.

"Yes, for what happened at Lady Turner's garden party. Now, if you are finished with the interrogation, I think it is time to rejoin the party." Alexandra's desire to not discuss Niall outweighed the fib she'd just told. Besides, soon it wouldn't matter anyway. He would be engaged to Lady Nerissa, and their friendship would change even more. She didn't want to lose him, their relationship. But, though he had assured her tonight that she wouldn't, she couldn't help but fear it. Sadness pounded against her heart, demanding attention as hot tears stung the corner of her eyes.

Don't cry, not here, not now.

Theodora took her hand and held it gently within her own as if sensing some of her inner turmoil. "We'd best get back inside."

Alexandra blinked away her tears, swallowed the hard lump in her throat, took in a deep breath, and set about pretending nothing had happened. It was how she'd been dealing with things as of late anyway. She feared that one day, very soon, she would explode from all the suppressed emotions that were trying to demand her attention.

No sooner had she reentered the ballroom than Lord Redford asked for her hand for the next set. The dance was pleasant, the music excellent, her partner one of the most sought-after men in attendance, and yet all she could think about was Niall. She knew she shouldn't, but his words, or rather that single word and then his quick retraction, had caught her off guard. This was Niall, one of her best friends. This was Niall, who had always been there for her. This was Niall . . .

He was intelligent and well-read, serious and shy, and so handsome. And he was promised to another, so she should not be thinking about him in that way. But now the thought had crept into her head, and she couldn't seem to stop it. She was being silly. There had been nothing to what he said. They were just friends. She was feeling emotional and thinking too much.

And just like that, the dance had ended and she had rejoined with her sisters and aunt. Had she performed the steps correctly? Had Lord Redford noticed how distracted she was? Oh, why could she not stop thinking about Niall?

He is your friend, and it is perfectly acceptable to think about friends, she reasoned unconvincingly. Thankfully the arrival of Miss Ashton and Lady Dorothy gave her a much-needed distraction.

"We saw you dancing with Lord Redford and just had to discover what he's like!" Miss Ashton exclaimed with the excitement of a wide-eyed miss. "He is quite handsome."

"He is very particular who he dances with. You're quite fortunate."

Lord Redford *was* handsome, but she didn't feel anything. "He is pleasant and a good dancer, but it is difficult to get to know gentlemen at these events." Her reply was simple and honest.

Was Lord Redford like so many other men of the *ton*, only interested in social standing and an heir, or would he be a husband in the full meaning of the word? And how would she know? All she really knew about him was that he spent time in gaming hells.

She was feeling all at sea and more than a little confused. Thankfully, her sisters and aunt didn't mind leaving, and no one seemed to notice their early departure, still too consumed as they were with the scene the Dowager Duchess of Blackburn had created a short time ago.

Once in the quiet of their rooms, the sisters recounted the evening's adventures.

"I saw Miss Raine rush up to you and then just as quickly leave. What was all that about?" Theodora asked.

Alexandra had completely forgotten about the note their friend had slipped into her hand. Reaching for her reticule, she retrieved the tightly folded paper. "Miss Raine writes that she overheard her brother and Lord Redford discussing an upcoming masque two days hence. Hosted by the famous courtesan Claudine de Beauregard."

This was the opportunity they'd been looking for. Surely, she would discover answers to her questions there. Her instinct warned that it was not a good idea to attend for fear of being discovered, but it was likely her last and best chance to delve into a forbidden part of society.

⁂

Chapter Eight

N IALL WAS ENJOYING a peaceful afternoon at home with his sister. Thankfully, their mother had gone out to visit friends. A serene calm washed over the bright and cheery drawing room. Since arriving in Town, days such as these had eluded him. He didn't want to think about duties and responsibilities. He didn't want to think about Lady Nerissa. And he certainly did not want to think about what he could not have.

Naomi was pre-occupied with her correspondence, while Niall reviewed the latest drawings for the new conservatory. He'd missed these quiet moments with his sister. Of his three sisters, he was closest with Naomi. Her temperament was nothing like his other sisters', or their mother's, for that matter.

Suddenly, a distant shriek disrupted the peace.

"What was that?" Naomi's head snapped up.

Another loud cry echoed from somewhere within the house. Niall rushed to the door just as his mother stormed in.

"How dare you go against my wishes," Mother yelled as she pointed at Naomi, whose face had turned an unsightly shade of red.

Niall steeled his nerves and prepared for battle. "Mother, why don't you calm down and—"

"I won't calm down." She stomped her foot in a most unladylike fashion. "I am still head of this house and—"

"No, I am head of this family," he firmly reminded her. "If you will explain what has distressed you, then perhaps we can resolve the issue."

She placed a dramatic hand to her temple, and with an equally dramatic sigh, bemoaned, "I have just returned from visiting Lady Jerome where I discovered your sister has disgraced this family most tragically."

He looked to his sister, who had buried her face in her hands and was trembling all over. He looked heavenward and prayed, *Give me strength.*

"What has she done?" he asked in a calm tone, hoping his mother would follow suit.

"She attended one of those . . . those . . ." She waved her hand frantically as if she could not bring herself to say the word. A moment later, she found the word. Several, in fact. "One of those *gatherings* the Grace sisters pretend is a salon and suitable for polite society, *and* after I forbade her from going."

"Mother," his sister began, "nothing inappropriate occurred. It was a pleasant afternoon spent in the company of friends."

"You were supposed to be resting in your room after claiming you had a headache and instead you snuck out, deceiving us all." Their mother was certainly laying on the guilt. "I know what goes on at that salon. It is all over Town how improper the conversation is, how they play childish games, and encourage impertinent behavior."

"Mother, I swear no such thing happened," Naomi cried into her hands, an age-old tactic she used to soften their mother's temper. Being the youngest, she usually succeeded. "Please don't be angry, Mama."

Naomi certainly had perfected her act, Niall would give her that. Their mother was already calming.

"Well, I suppose I can let it go this time, but mark my words, you shall have nothing to do with *those* sisters ever again." She glared harshly at Niall, as if he'd had something to do with the situation, then stormed out of the room.

He waited a moment to ensure their mother would not return to deliver a new tirade, which had happened before. Once he was certain she would not reenter, he went to the door and closed it.

"Now that we're alone, I expect you to tell me exactly why you snuck out." Niall also wanted to know if any of the things his mother had spewed about the goings-on at the Middleton residence were true, but he would tackle one issue at a time.

Deflated words rushed from her mouth. "Mother never lets me do anything I want to do. I'm always told who to converse with, what parties to attend. I . . . I just wanted to do something *I* wanted." Niall completely understood that reason. He'd felt it his whole life, and even more so as of late.

"I understand."

"You do?" Shock laced the two words.

"Yes. Now, would you care to tell me what *did* happen while you were there?"

He watched her features shift from calm to panic in the blink of an eye. "Nothing," she swallowed hard. He knew she was withholding the truth.

"Naomi?" He drew her name out with a firmness that made her cringe. "I will discover the truth sooner or later, and then—"

"Don't be angry with Alexandra or her sisters. They're just trying to help," she blurted out.

Too many questions raced through his mind. "Why . . . what . . . just trying to help?"

"Part of the salon is just as I told Mother, but . . ." She took in several deep breaths before continuing. "But after some of the ladies leave, a few stay behind to discuss things. I didn't stay. I promise. I came straight back home. But . . . Miss Ashton let it slip at Lord Grimsby's ball."

"What sort of things?" He had a suspicion he was not going to like the answer.

In a meek voice she answered, "Things that mothers don't

talk to us about." She lowered her voice even further. "When we marry."

Alexandra's questions.

Bloody hell, that was what she'd been doing? Gathering information to share with others? As if it weren't alarming enough that she'd asked or thought those things in the first place.

"Please say you're not angry," his sister pleaded.

Oh, he was beyond angry! At every turn, Alexandra was disrupting his senses and baiting the gossips.

"You will not go against Mother's wishes on this."

He needed to have a word, several in fact, with Alexandra.

So much for a pleasant day, he thought as he stormed from the house. He was going to pay a visit to Alexandra and put an end to her inappropriate salons before her or her sisters' reputations suffered.

He barely waited to be announced before he stormed into the parlor at Lady Middleton's house, disrupting Alexandra and Theodora who appeared to be deep in conversation.

"Theodora, could you please give His Grace and me a moment to speak?" Alexandra's voice was calm, without a hint of guilt.

Her sister eyed him with curiosity but didn't say a word as she departed the room, leaving the door open. If she was anything like Naomi, she would be listening just outside in the hallway.

Then, much to his surprise, Alexandra went to the door and closed it before turning around. Leaning against the door, she said, "I suspect this visit has something to do with your sister."

"My mother discovered her subterfuge. We were able to calm her down, but Naomi will certainly pay the price for her actions."

"Her actions?" Alexandra's voice raged, matching his rising temper. "What is so wrong about a gathering with friends and—"

The words stormed past his lips. "What the bloody hell do you think you're doing at your salon?"

"Talking. And it is none of your business."

"None of my . . . do you have any idea what the gossips are starting to say? What the gossips could say next? This affects my family, too."

"Men have their clubs. Why, then, can women not have a place of their own?" Alexandra argued. "Nothing unseemly has occurred and—"

"You do have a place. You have tea parties, shopping expeditions, jaunts in the park, and strolls." Niall's voice rumbled with anger. "What you're doing is vastly different to what's acceptable."

"Perhaps I don't want what's acceptable." She marched toward him, waving her hand as if declaring battle. "Perhaps I want to live by my own rules. Perhaps I want more than just tepid kisses. Perhaps I want passion and—"

Niall's rage and desire were at a tipping point. Without thought, he reached out and pulled her into his embrace. He could feel her heart pounding wildly against his chest, her breath coming in short spurts. Her lips were so close and yet so far away. He wanted to kiss her, wanted her to kiss him.

Her eyes were wide with shock yet hooded with desire. He fought to maintain control, to not give into the passion simmering between them. Time slowly ticked by in painful measure.

What was he doing?

He was holding the woman he had wanted for far too long against his chest. The warm, inviting scent of vanilla infiltrated his soul, demanding he take pleasure in her lips. He had to fight the urge to do what he wanted. He was promised to another.

"I . . . I think it best I go." His words brushed across her cheek.

"Yes, you should," she whispered but did not move.

Seconds passed as he fought between duty and desire, and in the end, duty won out. It always did. He detested that it did.

He inhaled deeply, taking in her scent one last time before stepping away. All words escaped him. She seemed to fight the same demons as he. Without further thought, he turned on his heel and left, never looking back. If he did, he would claim her as his own.

He stormed down the street, not in anger but in utter frustration. Instead of returning directly home, he went for a long walk, hoping that it would ease the tension that was wound so tight within that it threatened to snap at any moment.

He walked to the park, pacing the lengths of the various paths. What was he going to do about Alexandra? About his feelings for her?

Regret sank into his empty gut.

There was nothing he *could* do. But the question remained, how was he going to get her out of his mind? The only solution that came to him was to create distance. In doing so, it would mean that their friendship would be over. He didn't want to think about never seeing her again, never talking to her, never sharing his thoughts and ideas.

Perhaps he didn't need to end the friendship so abruptly. Perhaps distance alone would stamp down on his feelings. He would only see her when she was in Town, and before long, she would be a distant memory.

A couple of hours later he had ended his walk and returned home. He wasn't feeling any better, but he was expected to accompany his mother and sister to Mrs. Hadfield's ball. Naomi had informed him yesterday that Lady Wyner had been training her daughter-in-law to take over her position as one of the premier hostesses of the *ton*. One could say that tonight was Mrs. Hadfield's true coming out.

Minutes dragged into hours, but eventually, the appointed time to leave finally came. Although the carriage ride was silent, the tension within the dark interior screamed loud and clear.

Don't create scandal. Don't associate with the Grace sisters. Don't disgrace this family.

Would the *don'ts* ever go away?

Once they'd alighted the conveyance and were walking up

the grand staircase, Mother finally spoke. "I expect you to be on your best behavior, Naomi, perhaps even dancing with Lord Newland or Lord Neave this evening." What was it with his mother's obsession with gentlemen whose names began with the letter *N*? Was that the only requirement for a suitable match in Mother's world? She then turned her attention to him. "And I expect you to dance with Lady Nerissa. The *ton* needs to see what a splendid pair the two of you will make. And I will not tolerate any gossip tonight about either of you."

Her threat was empty. What would she do if gossip landed on her doorstep? Yell and scream? She'd already done that. The worst that would happen was a stern lecture punctuated by wails followed by another lecture about how displeased she was. They'd endured that time and again. Still, both he and his sister were of the same mind, that it was best to remain silent when she issued demands. They both nodded their heads then proceeded toward the grand ballroom.

Once inside, he saw Lady Nerissa conversing with Theodora. He wondered if Alexandra was dancing or . . . *Stop thinking about her.* He sucked in his breath, and instead of taking his usual spot near a column or against the wall, he went to Lady Nerissa.

Best to get his mother's request over and done with, otherwise he would never hear the end of it.

"Good evening, Lady Nerissa, Miss Theodora. I hope you are both well this evening." Perhaps it was his imagination, but a streak of guilt passed across Miss Theodora features. He knew her well enough to realize she was up to something. He would have to keep an eye on her. Now on to his first task. "Would you do me the honor of the next dance, Lady Nerissa?"

She took his offered arm, and he led her to where all the couples were waiting for the dance to begin. Tension coursed through his body, settling on his shoulders. The weight of his mother's demands, the impending announcement of his engagement, and the constant feeling that he was withering were tearing at his insides.

"It is a pleasant evening, is it not?" she questioned.

Her query brought him out of his dire musings. "Very pleasant, indeed." He had no clue what discuss with her. He knew her but really only in theory. He knew she was the daughter of a duke, that she was eighteen, and this was her first Season. But he had no idea what her likes and interests were, if she preferred Town or the quiet solitude of the country, or anything else. Her gaze pierced through his rambling thoughts, forcing him to focus on the present. "Are you enjoying the Season?"

"Oh, very much so." Excitement rushed past her smiling lips. "There are ever so many entertainments and diversions, and the company has been most pleasant." As they moved through the dance, she continued to praise everything about being in Town, but when Niall asked her if she enjoyed being in the country, her smile faded into a deep frown. "I do not enjoy the country. Not at all." Her statement was firm, final.

"And do you enjoy reading?"

"I simply adore poetry. Do you prefer Byron, Blake, or Shakespeare?"

"Truth be told, I do not care for poetry." His interests lay in more practical tomes.

Her features sagged and the spot between her brows crinkled as if she didn't quite understand his dislike for verse.

Perhaps if he could discover one thing they had in common, then marriage would not be so terrible. He thought about Naomi's interests and settled on the one they had shared. Most ladies of the *ton* could sketch or paint. "Do you enjoy drawing?"

She crinkled her nose in disgust. This was hopeless.

Silence enveloped them.

He'd never had any issues talking with Alexandra. The conversation always seemed to flow most naturally regardless of topics. She was without a doubt the most intelligent woman he knew. Even when she didn't understand a subject, she would ask questions, delve deeper. She seemed to have an insatiable desire for knowledge and truth. It was one of the things he found most attractive about her.

He and Lady Nerissa moved through the dance, each lost in their own thoughts. They were just too different. Despite what their families wanted, it was clear that he and she would not suit. He felt trapped and wondered if she felt the same. By the time the dance ended, both their moods had soured.

After returning Lady Nerissa to her mother, Niall took his usual place against the wall. He watched joyful couples dancing, ladies waving their fans as if being coy, and young gents trying to garner the attention of the fairer sex. And yet he still hadn't seen the one person he'd hoped to. He should be concentrating on keeping his distance from her, but for the life of him, he could not. He wanted to know if she was all right, enjoying the evening, and just . . . as miserable as he was.

Where was Alexandra? He'd seen both her sisters and Lady Middleton. Was she ill? Did she stay at home because of what had happened earlier in the day?

From across the room, he noticed his sister conversing with Theodora. Something seemed odd about their exchange, but he couldn't quite tell what. He continued to watch them for a few moments, and then Evelina appeared at Theodora's side, whispered something to her sister before they all scurried off in different directions.

He followed his sister. "Where are you sneaking off to?" he said once he was near enough.

Naomi whipped around, her breath coming in short spurts. "Niall, you startled me!"

He crossed his arms and surveyed her. "Would you care to tell me what you're up to?"

"Up to?" she swallowed hard. "Nothing." She looked this way and that, avoiding his eyes. Several seconds passed until she finally confessed. "Before Alexandra left, she made arrangements for me to have a moment with Mr. Norley."

His mind tried to wrap itself around what she'd said. There were two things wrong with her confession. One problem at a time. "What's this about Norley?"

"He is such a kind gentleman and I wanted to know him better, but since Mother doesn't approve, we can't even dance together without her scowling and worse. So, Alexandra arranged for us to meet in the music room and listen to Mrs. Hadfield sing. Mother doesn't care for such entertainments, so it is the only place—"

His sister's ramblings were causing his hair to stand on end. "I suppose I cannot object, just as long as you don't do anything worthy of gossip." He did like the gentleman, and although their mother would most arguably object to the match, he would not. His sole purpose for enduring this Season was to help Naomi find happiness.

She held up her hand. "I promise."

One problem solved, now on to the next.

"And would you care to explain where Alexandra went?"

Guilt flashed across her features. He knew he wouldn't like the answer, but he'd made a promise to watch over her, and he suspected she was getting into some sort of mischief. Hadn't he just been thinking about Alexandra's insatiable desire for the truth? And he knew what had been on her mind lately.

He continued to stare at his sister, waiting for her to reveal what she knew. As per usual, his patience won, and a moment later, she acquiesced. "She went to a masque. That's all I know."

"Why would she go to a masque when her sisters are here and—" Dammit. She wouldn't go to *that* masque, would she? "Do not, and I repeat do *not* do anything to set the gossips' tongues wagging. When Mother asks where I am, tell her I went to my club, nothing else."

Naomi nodded her head, her eyes wide with anxiety.

Without wasting another moment, Niall rushed from the ball. He only hoped he wasn't too late to save Alexandra's reputation.

ALEXANDRA WAS STILL confused after this afternoon's visit with Niall. Never in her life had she wanted Niall to kiss her more than at that moment. He was her childhood friend, and he was forbidden; soon he would belong to another. Perhaps that was why this evening was so important. She needed to finally discover the answers to her questions. Then perhaps she could find her own happiness.

She had arrived at Mrs. Hadfield's ball only to quickly claim a headache and beg to leave. She knew Lady Archibald, Aunt Imogene's friend who had come with them this evening, would gladly see her home. On the journey to the event, the lady had stated she was feeling under the weather and might not stay long. It was the excuse Alexandra had been hoping for.

After returning to her aunt's townhouse, she quickly changed again into her brother's old clothes—this time with a mask—checked her image in the mirror, and snuck out of the house.

Excitement coursed through her veins as she got into a hack. Thankfully, Claudine de Beauregard's abode, provided for her by an unnamed duke, wasn't far, and her flight went unseen. Alexandra had decided that she would spend less than an hour there, take in all she could, then return home, with no one the wiser.

Upon entering the opulent space, she noticed dozens of scantily clad women strolling around, enticing men. Seductive laughter flowed through the air, creating an atmosphere of indecency. She kept to the edge of the room, as she had at the gaming hell, but she hadn't made it far when all of a sudden, the room went still, and all sounds faded as several half-naked men marched into the room, instructing guests to move nearer toward the wall, creating a path and then standing sentinel.

"Gentlemen and gentlemen," one of the men began, then with dramatic fanfare announced, "the moment has come for you to view your hostess, Mademoiselle Claudine de Beauregard."

View your hostess? That was an odd choice of words, Alexandra thought to herself.

A hushed silence rippled across the group of attendees as four large men, their steps in precise time, slowly entered the room carrying what seemed to be a large silver platter hoisted upon their shoulders. Alexandra struggled to see what was happening. She backed up to the wall, and keeping one hand on it to steady herself, raised herself up high on tiptoe, hoping to catch a glimpse of what the people around her were gawking at.

Move your head! her inner voice shouted at the rather tall man in front of her. *This was hopeless.*

She moved farther along the wall, keeping to the shadows, until an opening in the crowd revealed itself. Once again, she raised herself up, straining to see what was on the silver—

She's naked! Mademoiselle Claudine de Beauregard is naked! She's naked and being carried in on a silver platter.

The words repeated over and over in her mind as her entire body felt as if it had gone up in flames.

A dozen beautiful women swayed into the room wearing thin drapes of the sheerest material she had ever seen. Their covering did not leave anything to the imagination. A roar of cheers and whistles reverberated around the room.

What sort of place was this?

She lowered herself, the tips of her toes aching from straining for so long. Could this evening get any worse?

A firm hand pulled at her arm, whipping her around, forcing her to come face to face with *worse.*

"Niall," she murmured. A sudden thrill shot through her veins before it collided with guilt.

Her body was pressed against his for the briefest of moments before he dragged her through the crowd toward a dark passageway. Even once they'd reached the corridor, he did not stop but traveled farther down it until the sounds of merriment softened to a dull hum. He went into a dark room and shut the door. He moved across the room to open the curtains just a sliver, and she caught the look of pure anger in his eyes. Waiting for the scold that was certain to come, she stood very still.

NIALL WAS LIVID. No, livid was too mild a word.

After he'd stormed out of the Hadfields' ballroom, he'd gone to his house to pick up a mask then rushed to Mademoiselle Beauregard's masque. It had been the talk of his club that the seductive courtesan was hosting an illicit soirée. Her events were notorious for excessive indulgences and debauchery—two things Niall had never participated in. Earlier, when his mother had asked what his plans for the evening were, attending the masque had never even entered his thoughts, and yet here he was, walking up the steps to the courtesan's establishment.

Men had congregated in the main hall and were making quite a commotion. Avoiding drawing attention to himself, he searched for Alexandra. With each breath he took, it seemed as if another dozen men poured into the room. The laughter, cheers, and whistles rose to deafening heights. Out of the corner of his eye, he spied the reason for all the noise. Mademoiselle Beauregard had made her entrance.

A quick flash of someone turning away caught his attention. *Alexandra.* Without further thought, he went to her side. Her men's attire did not conceal her voluptuous curves. In fact, it seemed to accentuate them. *Give me strength.* The only good thing was that she'd had the wherewithal to conceal her face, not to mention all the men present were too absorbed in the erotic display. That was to their advantage.

Grabbing her arm, he pulled her through the crowd toward the dark passageway. His only thoughts were to remove her from the immediate crowd and protect her identity. One of the unused side rooms would be as good a place as any to wait for the exit to clear.

"What the hell do you think you're doing?" he growled.

"Exploring and—"

"Damn it, Alexandra. Do you know what could happen?" He ran a frustrated hand through his hair. "I made a promise."

"Yes, I know," she huffed. "To Harold."

"And to your father." If Lord Grace were alive, what would he have had to tell him? *Your daughter thought it a lark to explore an infamous courtesan's house.* The rage within was building, mixing with other emotions he dared not entertain.

"My father?"

He ignored her question. "I cannot believe you thought this a good idea."

"No one recognized me."

"But someone *could* have—someone should have!—and then what?" He tried to control his temper as he sought answers. "What are you even doing here?"

"Discovering the truth," Alexandra stated in a defiant tone as she raised her chin.

"The truth?"

"Yes, about men."

Niall was quickly losing his patience. "The truth about men? What kind—"

"I'm sure you have noticed, being one, that men behave quite differently when they are not under the scrutiny of the grande dames. I simply want to understand why that is."

"They do not—"

"How are we supposed to know what to do, how to please our husbands?"

Heat rose through his body. He cleared his throat, trying not to imagine Alexandra pleasing—. "They will show you," his voice cracked. He was quickly losing control.

He could not believe he was having this conversation with her. It was improper. No, not just improper, it was inappropriate, unseemly, ungentlemanly even, and entirely . . . arousing.

"Oh, and I suppose the reason that Lord Botte, Lord Shepard, Mr. Bacon, and Mr. Nesbitt are present is not because their wives are unable to satisfy them, but for an entirely different and altogether innocent reason." The thick sarcasm in her voice would have been amusing if not for the topic they were discussing. She continued her rant. "It seems to me that wooing is what matters most to men. Once said gentleman wins the hand—or rather, the dowry—of the fair maiden, then he is free to find comfort elsewhere."

"Any of these so-called *gentlemen* could have their way with you and you would never even see it coming."

AND THAT WAS precisely the problem—Alexandra *didn't* understand. She was on a quest for knowledge and there was no turning back, but she wasn't certain, based on the scowl Niall wore, that he would enlighten her. However, it was worth asking—she had little left to lose. "But that's just *it*—"

"What is just *it?*" Niall slashed through her question with gritted teeth.

"What does that mean exactly?"

"What does what—"

It was her turn to interrupt him. With a stomp of her foot, she demanded, "Have their way with me. What does it mean when—"

One moment she was demanding an answer to her question, and the next, she was being pushed against the closed door by firm, masculine flesh and kissed by the only man she'd ever truly desired.

She desired Niall. That realization slapped her hard across the face.

Without a second thought, she wrapped her arms around his neck, pulling herself closer to him, wanting to feel every inch of his body. She'd been so determined to think of him as no more than a friend, and yet here she was, kissing him.

It was the most glorious moment of her life and yet she knew it couldn't last.

Niall must have realized the same. He eased back from her, his forehead pressed gently against hers. "I shouldn't have done that." He brushed a soft kiss to her temple.

"No, you shouldn't have." Alexandra kissed the sensitive spot at the base of his neck.

"I'm promised to Lady Nerissa." He kissed her cheek.

"I know." Alexandra sighed as she kissed his chin.

"Alexandra." Her name whispered past his lips in a most seductive tone that sent tingles through her body. "I've always wanted to kiss you."

Alexandra pulled back and saw heart-rending tenderness in his deep green eyes. "You have?"

"Hell and damnation, you're all I think about, all I have ever thought about. But I can't . . ." He sucked in a deep, shuddered breath, then lowered his head and took her lips in a sweet, tender kiss. The kind of kiss Alexandra suspected meant *goodbye*.

"Let me take you home."

Somehow he managed to get her out of the house and to Aunt Imogene's without anyone detecting them. And somehow, she held in her tears, hiding the despair even from her sisters as she entered their private parlor.

"What did you discover?" Theodora asked with excited anticipation. "I thought you would be gone longer."

She couldn't very well be honest with them, tell them that not only had Niall discovered her subterfuge, but he'd also kissed her. Not only kissed her, but stirred the desire that she'd always hoped for though she knew they could never be. She rubbed the spot on her chest just above where her heart was breaking.

"It was not quite what I was expecting." That was the absolute truth. She had not anticipated seeing Mademoiselle Beauregard carried in on a platter, or pure lust that flowed like water, and she most certainly had not expected to be kissed by Niall. "I don't think we're going to get the answers we desire from a place like that." It was a venue where men went to avoid their wives, perhaps even forget about them for a while. It was an establishment for men to indulge in their desires and justify their actions.

Evelina and Theodora glanced at one another and then looked at Alexandra. She could not tolerate any more questions this evening.

"I'm going to bed. We can talk in the morning." And with that, she retreated to her room.

She was going to hell, there was no doubt in her mind about it. She'd kissed Niall, but he was promised to another, the announcement expected any day. She'd kissed him!

She plopped into bed and pulled the covers up over her head, forcing the outside world away. She wanted time to reflect, to remember the feel of his hand on the small of her back, the touch of his cheek against hers. What was she going to do? Could she go to her aunt? Aunt Imogene might get upset with Alexandra's subterfuge. Would she blame Evelina and Theodora too? Perhaps she would be able to discuss her conundrum—not all the details, of course—with the ladies. She could pose *what-if* questions and see what advice they had to offer.

And then there was his odd comment about making a promise to her father. When did that happen, and *what had been promised*?

There were so many confusing thoughts swirling through her mind and heart that she could not focus on a single one. What was she to do?

Chapter Nine

THE NEXT DAY brought with it more chaos and uncertainty. Alexandra had been on tenterhooks waiting for their special salon and the opportunity to pose her questions to the ladies. Most of their usual guests remained after their regular salon, but they hadn't yet begun their discussion for the afternoon when an unexpected visitor joined them.

"Lady Dorothy and Lady Nerissa have just arrived, Miss Grace," Roger, Aunt Imogene's butler, announced.

Alarms rang in Alexandra's head. Lady Nerissa had never attended one of their salons before. Not even the proper one!

She knew.

Somehow, Lady Nerissa must have found out what transpired between her and Niall last night and had come to confront her.

"I didn't think you would mind Lady Nerissa joining us today," Lady Dorothy said as they entered. "She's a dear friend and has quite the conundrum."

Alexandra had completely forgotten the two were such good friends. Oh, how had life got so complicated?

"Good afternoon, Lady Nerissa," she said with all the politeness she could muster through her guilt. Out of the corner of her eye, she spied Evelina's concerned look. Both her sisters were far too perceptive for their own good. She knew there would be questions, but what was she to tell them? That she'd fallen in love with . . . ?

Oh, dear, I'm in love with Niall.

Pushing her rambling thoughts away, she turned her attention to their guest. "It is most pleasant of you to join us. I believe you're acquainted with Miss Ashton and Miss Raine."

As they settled into their seats, she could not help feeling anxious as nervous tension tightened the muscles in her neck. What if Lady Nerissa were here to accuse her of having feelings for Niall? How would she deny that?

Evelina must have sensed her uneasiness as she took control of the gathering. "We're going to discuss—"

"I want to know more," Lady Nerissa interrupted. And then she blurted out, "My engagement is to be announced in the coming week and whenever I'm near . . ." She paused for a moment then continued in a hushed tone, "*him*, I cannot utter two coherent words. I truly don't know what to do! I cannot even imagine what I will be like once we marry and we're alone!" She was practically in tears by the time she ended her rambling.

"Who are you engaged to?" Miss Ashton asked the question that was on everyone's mind.

Well, everyone's except Alexandra's.

She'd known about the forced engagement for several years, ever since Niall had confessed his troubles to her one spring afternoon. He'd been upset after yet another argument about it with his mother, only that time, his elder sisters had also swarmed over him with pronouncements about what they believed to be best for his life. Alexandra remembered being amazed at his strength and fortitude to always do right for duty's sake. She'd always admired his dedication to family, too.

She tried not to worry her lip as she waited for Lady Nerissa to answer. Was this when she would accuse Alexandra of stealing her beloved?

"I cannot say. We promised not to tell anyone until the time came, but I don't know who to turn to. Lady Dorothy suggested I come here. I do want to be a good wife, but when I tell my mother my concerns, she just tells me it's normal and to do my duty. But what does that mean?"

It seemed as if they all had the same questions and received the same results when they sought answers.

Alexandra knew she could not have a future with Niall, regardless of the kiss they'd shared, or how he'd stirred a desire within her that she hadn't even known she possessed. And never mind how her heart was breaking and that all she wanted to do was curl up in a ball and cry. She could still ensure he had a happy future with Lady Nerissa. She had to put her feelings aside and help the other girl.

She forced the lump down in her throat, went to Lady Nerissa's side, and soothed, "You needn't worry. Although we are inexperienced as well, we have joined together to discover more about the intimacies between men and women. We may not have many answers yet, but we are friends. You are welcome to join us in our quest for knowledge."

"Really?" Lady Nerissa sniffled several times. "His Gr . . . I mean *he* has often spoken highly of you and your sisters, and now I see why."

It touched her heart to know Niall thought so well of them.

"What questions do you have? Perhaps we can answer a few," Theodora said.

"I guess the most important at the moment is, how do you kiss a man?" Lady Nerissa clenched her hands anxiously. "We've had moments alone—well, not quite alone—but he's never expressed any desire to want to kiss me. Perhaps he does not think me pretty or accomplished or—"

"Perhaps he is just being a gentleman." Evelina was always the practical-minded one.

"I once spied one of our maids with a footman. His hands were all over her body, touching . . ." Lady Nerissa shook her head as if in shock at what she was saying. "He was not handsome, and yet, she was succumbing to his attentions. There has to be more than just someone's appearance."

The answering words poured from Alexandra's mouth as if they were the most natural in the world. "It's the way he makes you feel, as if you're the only woman in the world he wants to be with at that moment. When his breath caresses your cheek and your pulse races as you wait in anticipation for the moment when his lips will finally meet yours. And then—"

Theodora's excited interruption broke through the words she hadn't realized she'd said out loud. "Alexandra Josephina Grace! Have you been kissed?"

She couldn't very well tell them that she had kissed Niall just last night, especially not with his fiancée sitting in the same room. Her cheeks heated as she fumbled for words. "No . . . I . . . I overheard one of the debutantes at Lady Evans' ball."

She was most certain that neither of her sisters accepted her flimsy excuse, but the rest of the guests seemed satisfied with it, for the moment at least.

"I just knew coming here was the right decision," Lady Nerissa announced with confident enthusiasm.

Alexandra was not surprised when, after all the ladies had departed, her sisters cornered her, wanting information.

"Now that we're alone, are you going to tell us who you kissed?" Theodora practically begged.

"No."

"So, you have been kissed," Evelina stated.

She could not keep denying what had happened between her and Niall. Her sisters would work it out on their own sooner or later, probably sooner. She sucked in her breath, then attempted to pacify them for the time being. "I can neither confirm nor deny any such thing occurred—"

"Alexandra," Theodora enunciated every syllable of her name with a firm scold. "You're nigh impossible at times."

She shook her head, about to argue, when Evelina chimed in, "Then at least tell us who Lady Nerissa was referring to?"

She hedged. "If the rumors are to be believed—"

"We've heard the rumors, too." Evelina pointed to herself and Theodora. "And, I do not believe for one moment they have formed a *tendre* for each other."

Her sisters were relentless this afternoon. She was not prepared to tell them all she knew. Niall had confided in her years ago, and she'd promised to never reveal his family's scheme to marry him off to the daughter of a friend. She knew she could trust her sisters and she truly detested lying to them, but she'd made that vow to Niall.

So caught up in her own musings was she that she did not notice the intense stares from both her sisters. Words swirled through her mind, but none reached her lips.

"When you're ready to talk, we're here for you," Theodora said as both her sisters took her in an embrace.

Alexandra knew the time was quickly approaching when Niall's engagement to Lady Nerissa would be announced and she would need her sisters then, more than she ever had, she suspected, if the current ache weighing her down was any indication.

EVER SINCE THE kiss, things had been awkward between herself and Niall. She'd seen him at a few events, but neither of them had seemed able to keep eye contact. Talking to one another was impossible. And yet, he always seemed to be nearby.

Alexandra's heart sank, its lining cracking a little more with each passing day and the knowledge that soon he would be engaged to another. She missed him. She missed the casual flow of conversation they'd once shared, and worse, she desperately missed the feel of his lips on hers.

She was certain that tonight would hold more of the same: unstimulating dinner conversation with someone she was forced to sit next to, awkward glances from across the table, men imbibing brandy and rowdy conversation while the women discussed the latest *on dits*. It was all too ordinary and exhausting. She longed for the country, for dinner amongst friends filled with conversation about art and architecture. There were no pretenses, no ulterior motives, just good companionship.

By the time the hour came, and she and her family entered Lady Pynes's drawing room, Alexandra was already eager to return to her aunt's home. Her head was aching, and her stomach was churning for reasons she could not—or would not—name.

Theodora and Evelina mumbled something about talking to someone, then took their leave, leaving her to stand awkwardly next to her aunt, who was completely engrossed in conversation with Lady Archibald.

She edged away from her relative and moved toward the elegant harp standing sentinel at the far end of the large drawing room. It was a beautiful instrument, and the only thing she looked forward to this evening was listening to Lady Carol, Lady Pynes's daughter, play. Even with her back toward the entry, her body knew the moment Niall entered. She desperately wanted to go to him, to confide her feelings, to . . .

Stop. You must stop thinking about him.

A short time later, dinner was announced and progressed like clockwork. All the while, Niall kept glancing her way, unsettling her nerves and setting her pulse aflame. Oh, why did her heart have to reveal itself when there was nothing that could be done about it? She was thankful that Lady Nerissa was not present this evening. Seeing them together would have surely done her in.

By the time the men rejoined the ladies after their brandy, and everyone gathered to listen to Lady Carol play, Alexandra's nerves were completely raw. Although she did not want to miss the performance, she needed a moment to regain her composure.

With the guests already assembled in the drawing room, she was able to make a quiet escape. She'd visited Lady Carol on several occasions and knew the day parlor was just along the hallway.

Minutes later, she was alone, the chilly space cooling her heated face. She went to the window and pulled back one curtain just enough to allow a stream of moonlight to enter. She glanced upwards at the full moon, hypnotized by its beauty.

"I was hoping to find you alone," Niall's voice swept through the room, reaching her heart. She slowly turned around, preparing her words, then she noticed his slumped shoulders and sad features. Before she could ask what the matter was, he spoke, "I wanted to apologize for the other night. I should not have . . ." He seemed to struggle with his words. "I never meant—"

"I know," she said. It had been the most glorious, but also the worst, moment of her life, for she'd discovered just how much she loved him, and yet she could never express those feelings.

They stood, frozen, a dozen feet apart. It might as well have been an ocean.

"I should return—"

"What promise did you make to my father?" This would probably be the only opportunity she would ever have to ask him. Once he was married, he would be out of her life forever. A fierce pain struck her heart. She swallowed hard, hoping to ease the ache.

He pushed his spectacles further up his nose. "That I would protect you and your sisters."

It seemed a simple enough promise, but why hadn't Papa made that request of their brother, or had he already lost faith in Harold?

"When?"

"Alexandra, it may be too painful—"

"I want to know." It didn't matter if it was too painful, this very moment was already just that. She wanted to know the truth.

He took a step closer but did not close the distance. "It was in the early days of his illness. I happened across your father while on my early morning ride. I was surprised to see him on foot and so far from Charis Hall. He didn't seem himself, so I offered to walk with him to the house." He paused for a moment, watching Alexandra, as if ensuring she was all right.

She offered a reassuring nod. "I think I remember that morning. Theodora was beside herself with worry because he couldn't be found. After that day, she decided he needed companionship during the night and stated that she would watch over him during those dark hours, wandering the halls with him, comforting him." Up until his dying day, her dearest papa always had something to say. "What did you talk about?"

"You and your sisters. He was worried about who would watch over his three precious girls when he met your mother in heaven."

Tears stung her eyes as the words were absorbed into her heart. For as long as she could remember, Papa always called her and her sisters his precious girls. Oh, how she wished she could hear that sweet endearment from him just one more time. Then something dawned on her. "Did he not believe Harold would take his brotherly duties seriously?"

Niall shook his head and let out a long sigh. "He didn't remember he had a son."

"Oh," she whispered. She hadn't realized that his mind had slipped quite so much in those early days. It had been heartbreaking to watch him lose his memory. She looked at Niall. "So, he asked you to protect us?"

"No," he said as he started to move closer, then stopped. "I told him it would be an honor to watch over his precious girls."

"And you always have," she said with all the love she felt but could not express. Niall had always been there for her and her sisters, regardless of their escapades.

"And I always will." He took another step closer, and she realized he was struggling with the same thoughts she was. There was so much they wanted to say but were not at liberty to speak of. "I have cherished every minute of our friendship."

"I have too." She wanted nothing more than to rush into his arms, be held by him, be kissed by him. "I have no regrets about the other night." She would always have that one perfect kiss.

"I—"

The sound of applause drifted in from the corridor, breaking the moment.

He sucked in his breath as he took a step back. "I should go."

And once again, he walked out of her life.

Chapter Ten

I**T HAD BEEN** a miserable couple of days. The weather had been blustery and dreary, and the evening events lacking. If not for their afternoon salon, the sisters would have gone mad with boredom. Although at least they had each other for entertainment.

That still hadn't kept Alexandra from festering over the impending news of Niall's engagement to Lady Nerissa. Her feet ached from all the pacing, her eyes were tired and sore from the lack of sleep and the constant tears that stung them. And her heart . . . she'd never known that one's heart could actually feel as if it had shattered into pieces.

Don't think about what cannot be!

She shifted her concentration back to the book in her hand but kept reading the same passage over and over. Perhaps once the news of his engagement was announced, in time she would find peace and the strength to think about the future. Certainly, time would heal a broken a heart, and perhaps, eventually, she could even think about her own marriage prospects.

The problem was, no gentleman—other than the one she could never be with—had ever caught her eye, not even for a breath of a moment. A long inner sigh quavered through her body. What was she to do? *It's time to let go of him.*

Just then, Evelina stormed into the parlor—with Theodora following close behind—her cheeks flushed with anger, breaking through Alexandra's grim musings. "It finally happened."

"What happened?" Alexandra questioned.

"Those old biddies just had to write about our salon." Evelina handed the gossip sheet to Alexandra. "And, might I add, it is not very well written." She plopped down on the sofa next to Theodora.

Alexandra strolled toward the window, her back toward her sisters as she pushed her own troubles aside. This was a good, albeit unwanted distraction. Sucking in a deep breath, she focused on the current predicament. Hazy sunlight streaked across the page, highlighting the short snippet. "Thankfully, it doesn't mention us by name, but it does make quite a few references to the—and I quote—inappropriate topics of conversation, and how the ladies in question believe they can do whatever they want without consequences."

"This is not good! What are we to do?" Theodora asked with concern. "If we're discovered, many of our attendees may suffer as well."

"We won't be discovered. Clearly, one of the ladies who attends cannot be trusted. We will simply have to reorganize and take a different approach."

"Wouldn't it be brilliant if those gossips had to write something good about us?" Evelina said with a laugh. "Although I'm certain it would still be poorly written."

Alexandra started to pace as she inwardly rolled her eyes. Sometimes, all Evelina could think about was the written word.

"I have an idea." She turned to face her sisters. "We will simply start some gossip of our own. At the next ball, we need to make sure we're overheard." She paced back and forth several times more, working the details out in her head. "Evelina, you will pen a love letter between . . ." She waved her hand about. "Oh, just make up some silly words that any couple might say to each other. You will leave it in the ladies' retiring room but will be sure not to be seen. We have to make certain that the rumormongers stumble across our clues. That should distract from us."

"Perhaps I can help," Aunt Imogene said as she strolled into the parlor, startling the girls. "Oh, you can wipe those shocked expressions off your faces. I may appear to be in my dotage, but I assure you it's all a ruse. How else am I to have fun? And don't you think for one moment I did not know what the three of you were getting up to at your salon."

Alexandra swallowed hard, trying to cover the true intention of their gathering. "Aunt Imogene, we would never—"

She waved her hand in dismissal. "You three are just like your mother. Far too inquisitive at times." She offered warm smile that touched Alexandra's heart. "And I wouldn't have it any other way. Now, let's get to work."

ALEXANDRA SPENT AN enjoyable afternoon with her sisters and Aunt Imogene plotting their course of action. Evelina wrote a love note—a poorly written one at that, so as to throw off the scent of their subterfuge. The plan was simple but, according to their aunt, infallible.

With the plan set in motion, everyone readied for the evening. Alexandra was thankful that the event at which they'd chosen to enact their scheme was Lady Holland's extravagant ball. The crush would make moving about the crowds and spying a simpler task.

A few hours later, they arrived at Lady Holland's ball. It was a lovely sight to behold. Bright colors, the scent of fragrant flowers, and mischievous laughter all swirled about the grand room, but then all of a sudden, the place quieted as an exceptionally handsome man strolled into the room with all the confidence of a Greek god.

"Who's the gentleman?" Evelina questioned their aunt with interest.

"That is Lord Raine. He is without a doubt the most notorious rake there ever was."

"That is Miss Raine's brother!" Evelina exclaimed a little too loudly, for those around them turned and eyed their small group. She quickly clamped her mouth shut. It was quite unlike her sister to be discomposed by the sight of a handsome man. However, Evelina would never tolerate the ways of a rake.

Aunt Imogene leaned in, ready to share what knowledge she had about Lord Raine. "From what Lady Archibald told me just this afternoon, his mother is quite troubled that he has no intention of marrying, and she has insisted that he chaperone his sister for the remainder of the Season. And no one says *no* to Lady Raine."

"She sounds like a dreadful woman," Evelina said. "I feel sorry for the poor lady who enters that family."

"Lady Raine *is* perhaps one of the most dreadful women I've encountered. How in heaven her daughter is as pleasant and cheerful as she is, I will never know." Aunt Imogene tsked several times, then continued. "Are my girls ready to enact the plan?"

My girls. The endearment settled in Alexandra's aching heart and soothed some of the pain she'd been experiencing over the past days. It was good to be part of a loving family.

The three sisters nodded their heads in unison. This was the most fun they'd had all Season. Theodora was to circle the ballroom, distracting any would-be gossips, especially Lady Shepard, who had been sniffing around their business at every event they'd attended. Alexandra was to keep watch from her post on the mezzanine landing, which provided an excellent view of the entire ballroom. Aunt Imogene was to follow Evelina, who would leave the love note in the ladies' retiring room, standing guard at the entry to the corridor. Once the task was completed, Aunt Imogene was to play the encouraging chaperone, securing a dance for her niece.

They each took their positions. If tonight was a success, they planned to leave a similar note at the next ball. They'd determined that they would only place missives at crowded events such as this, where it would be difficult to determine who had "lost" the love note.

It had already been nearly twenty minutes and her aunt and sister had not yet returned. With each passing minute Alexandra's anxiety rose. Theodora had taken yet another turn around the ballroom. Soon, those present who were of a more observant nature might begin to suspect something was amiss. She was beginning to think their plan had failed.

Five more minutes, then I will . . .

She would what? What was she to do? Discover if Theodora heard any gossip? She couldn't very well rush about without someone noticing. And what if she missed something—what, she could not fathom, but something—while she went to Theodora? No, it was better to stay put and trust in her relatives' abilities.

She was still arguing with herself when Aunt Imogene came into view, then casually strolled toward the grand staircase, making her way toward Alexandra.

She attempted nonchalance as Aunt Imogene joined her, but clearly failed as the words rushed from her mouth. "What happened? Was she discovered?"

"No, of course not," Aunt Imogene replied as if Alexandra's concerns were the most preposterous thing she'd ever heard. She leaned in and spoke for Alexandra's ears only. "Lady Shepard cornered us the moment we entered the corridor and was digging about for any gossip. I planted the seed, but Evelina could not very well complete her task just then. However, all is well now."

"Oh, thank heaven," Alexandra said with a sigh of relief. She scanned the ballroom, but a dance had just begun, making it difficult to spot her sister in the crush. "Where is Evelina?"

"Dancing with Lord Raine." Alexandra stared at her relative. That sort of man was the last type her sister would ever want to dance with. She was just about to say as much when Aunt

Imogene stated, "She could not very well refuse him, not without creating gossip."

She supposed her aunt was correct.

"We should rejoin the crush below," her relative prompted.

Alexandra was enjoying her current spot. Although not quiet or peaceful, she was away from the crowd. But she supposed she'd hidden long enough.

Soon after they returned to the main area, her aunt had scurried off to talk to a friend, and Theodora was engaged in conversation with Miss Ashton. Alexandra walked along the perimeter of the room, watching Evelina dance while listening for any gossip.

"Miss Jerome discovered a note on the floor in the ladies' retiring room."

The mention of the note brought Alexandra to a halt. She quickly took a spot against the wall behind an obliging vase set on a pedestal.

"What did it say?" She did not recognize the voice of the woman who asked the question.

"It would seem there is a clandestine affair afoot." *That* voice she did recognize. *Lady Mavis.*

"Between?" the other woman asked with anxious excitement.

"Names are not mentioned, but they refer to themselves as *cabbage* and *potato.*"

"Cabbage and potato? My word, are they lovers or preparing soup? I wonder who they could be? Do you think there is a connection to the Graces' salon?"

Alexandra held her breath. This was the moment of truth. Had their plan worked?

"No." Relief coursed through Alexandra with that single word. "Lady Shepard believes it is between a debutante and a fortune hunter."

"Well, if anyone could work out who the couple is, it is Lady Shepard."

Alexandra strained to hear their next words as they giggled

then strolled away. At least their plan was a success. Not wanting to be asked to dance, she kept to her slightly hidden spot behind the pedestal and was looking about for her sisters when she spied Niall conversing with Lady Nerissa. His mother and Lady Nerissa's mama were keeping close watch over the couple.

A fierce pang struck her heart. This is how it would forever be. She would never be able to confide in him, be comforted by him . . . be kissed by him. Damn pesky tears threatened her resolve once again. She'd known this day would come, but why did it have to hurt so much?

"Argh!" Evelina's exasperation startled her, breaking through her anguish. "Without a doubt, he is the most infuriating man to ever walk the earth!"

"Who—"

"Lord Raine! He may be an excellent dancer and charming, but he certainly puts on airs about everything!" With each word her sister spoke, her voice rose and her cheeks reddened.

"Perhaps we—"

"By Zeus!" Theodora cried as she rushed to their side, followed by Miss Jerome.

This was not good.

"Good evening, Miss Jerome," Alexandra stated with all the pleasantness she could muster.

Miss Jerome shrugged her shoulders with an air of superiority. "I know you know something. The three of you are always up to something untoward. Now, tell me," she demanded.

Alexandra could sense Evelina's temper rising. It didn't surface often, but when it did, few were safe. She grabbed her sister's hand, pulling her slightly back and took control of the situation. "Whatever are you referring to?"

"The note."

"Did you send us a note? I apologize, but we did not receive—"

"Not from me," Miss Jerome said with a huff of annoyance. "The love letter that was discovered earlier this evening in the ladies' retiring room."

Theodora looked to Alexandra, her eyes wide with uncertainty over how to handle the situation.

She gave her youngest sister a little shake of her head then addressed the gossip. "I am not aware of any letter. My sisters and I have been in the ballroom the entire evening. In fact, Evelina and I were just commenting on how stuffy it is. Of course, she's just danced with Lord Raine and—"

"Lord Raine is in attendance?" Miss Jerome practically swooned, but thankfully decided to reserve a complete faint for the presence of said lord.

"Yes," Evelina said, barely containing her disdain for the rake.

Miss Jerome's interrogation was done and her attention now on a different task. Without a further word, she took her leave.

"Hopefully she'll forget about her suspicions about us and the love letter," Theodora said.

"I highly doubt that," Evelina stated with sarcasm. "But it should give us some time."

Out of the corner of her eye, Alexandra spied Niall gliding across the dance floor with Lady Nerissa. They looked far too lovely together. A fierce pang struck her heart as hot tears stung the corners of her eyes.

Please don't cry, not here, not now!

She bit the inside of her cheek, hoping to shift the pain away from her wounded heart. She'd told herself to let go and yet her heart wasn't ready. Would the pain of seeing them together ever subside? She truly did not know how much more she could take this evening. "I think it best we call it an evening."

Without words, Evelina took one of her hands, Theodora the other. Alexandra did not know if her sisters suspected her inner turmoil, but it was comforting to have them beside her. As a unified trio, they left the ballroom in search of their aunt. Let the gossips wag their tongues. The Grace sisters were above their tittle-tattle.

Chapter Eleven

"IT's A SUCCESS!" Aunt Imogene rushed into the sisters' private parlor, scandal sheet in hand.

The sisters jumped up at the same time and rushed to their relative's side. Theodora took the sheet from her aunt and began to read, "A certain young lady, who goes by the name Cabbage, has created quite a scandal for her family, for one of high birth does not associate with those found in the dirt, namely the potato." Theodora paused, scanning the rest of the sheet. "That's it. Nothing about us or the salon."

"What is our next step?" Evelina said.

"I think we should wait a couple of days. We don't want to raise eyebrows. Let those gossips simmer over this for a while," Aunt Imogene suggested. She waved her hand with enthusiasm. "I have it. The next time I visit Lady Archibald, I will inquire after the latest *on dits*, and slip in some other *gossip* that I overheard about Cabbage and Potato. I just know she will take the bait. Mildred cannot resist a good piece of gossip."

"That's an excellent idea. We can also enlist some of the ladies from the salon to help," Theodora said.

"Hmmm, I think we need to be careful. We still don't know who tattled," Evelina stated.

"I think you're right." Alexandra paced back and forth for a moment, her sisters and aunt watching. "For the time being, we should not discuss our usual topics at the other salon. We need to throw them off the scent while determining who we can trust."

"But first, we need to ready for our afternoon promenade."

A short time later, Alexandra, along with her sisters and aunt, was enjoying a pleasant ride in the open carriage. It seemed as if all of London had descended upon Hyde Park to enjoy the fine afternoon. It was a nice distraction from the turbulence that had disrupted her of late. If only Niall weren't promised to another. A hard lump grew in her throat. *Don't think about him*, she begged her mind. But how could she not when Niall was never far from her thoughts? *Just enjoy the day.*

"There's Lord Raine," Evelina said with exasperation as she rolled her eyes.

"He does cut quite a fine figure on that horse," Aunt Imogene commented. She almost sounded like a silly schoolgirl. "He certainly would never do as a husband, unless he could be reformed." The older woman leaned in and, on a giggle, added, "Reformed rakes make the best husbands in the bedroom."

"Aunt Imogene!" Alexandra and Evelina exclaimed in unison.

Alexandra could not believe her aunt just said *that* in public, where anyone might overhear.

"I have so many questions," Theodora said with enthusiasm as she tilted her head.

Alexandra leaned forward, too, and in a hushed tone, said, "Perhaps we should wait until we return home. There are eyes and ears everywhere." Just then, she spied Miss Jerome and her mother in the carriage nearest to theirs. Of course, those two were notorious gossips, and the sisters did not need to give them any cud to chew.

"Oh, good afternoon, Lady Middleton, Miss Grace, Miss Evelina, and Miss Theodora. Isn't it a pleasant day? And so many people. I can't help but wonder if Miss Cabbage is present?" Miss Jerome eyed their party as if hoping to catch them in a lie.

"As a matter of fact, I overhead one of the passersby say they believed they saw Miss Cabbage and Mr. Potato strolling . . ." Aunt Imogene paused dramatically then continued, "*without* a chaperone, down near the Serpentine."

Their aunt certainly had a way with words. Alexandra had greatly underestimated her. She was learning to appreciate and understand her relative in a way she never had before. She couldn't help but wonder about the adventures Imogene had had through the years. She suspected her life had been quite exciting.

Miss Jerome seemed entirely too interested in Aunt Imogene's tale. She always had been a tittle-tattler, but this interest in others' downfalls was somewhat alarming. Reminiscences from the past tickled Alexandra's thoughts. Although they had been careful not to say too much in front of Miss Jerome, or Lady Mavis, for that matter. She suspected that the former was more perceptive than she'd first realized and was responsible for exploiting the sisters' salon for her own social advancement. Well, she would just have to throw Miss Jerome off the scent even more. And there was one man Alexandra knew of who could use a little scandal in his life, especially after he'd tried to blackmail Miss Ashton into marrying him last Season. Not to mention that he'd had the audacity to reenter society this Season with all the pomp and arrogance of a rake, scoundrel, and rogue intertwined into one.

"I have often wondered if a certain notorious rake, whose recent return to Town, is somehow connected to these letters."

Miss Jerome gasped as she clasped her hand to her chest. "You don't mean Mr. Markham? I hadn't considered him," she said, instantly coming to her own conclusions. "It would be just like him to try and seduce a reputable lady of the *ton* and then leave her to face the scandal on her own."

Alexandra's plan was working better than she thought it would. Not only had Miss Jerome taken the bait, but she had single-handedly concocted an entire tale.

"Well, if anyone can save Cabbage's reputation, it is me," Lady Jerome added. "Thank you, ladies." And with that, mother and daughter went on their way.

A few moments passed before her youngest sister commented with a giggle, "I wonder how Mr. Markham will react when he learns that he is Potato?"

"It will be an improvement on how he's been recently referred to," Aunt Imogene said. Then quickly added, "Just to clarify, I do not usually spread rumors, but I do enjoy the undoing of those who deserve it."

"Now, on to more important matters. Why exactly do reformed rakes make the best husbands?" Theodora said, revisiting the topic from only a short time ago.

"Theodora, you shouldn't ask such a thing in view of so many," Evelina scolded in a hushed yet firm tone.

"Now is as good a time as any," Aunt Imogene informed them. She looked this way and that, then leaned forward once more, expecting the sisters to do the same, forming a tighter circle of confidence. "Reformed rakes make the best lovers. They're quite practiced in the art of intimacy." The older woman rendered the three of them absolutely speechless. And then she shocked them even more. "I may not have enjoyed being married, but I have enjoyed other pleasures."

Alexandra shook her head. Why did women have to talk in riddles? "I have so many questions, I don't know where to start."

"I will tell you what I told your mother before she married your father. Never be afraid of desire or passion."

That was what Mother had written to them.

Alexandra wanted to return to the house and reread the letters her mother had left for them. She suspected they contained more insight than they first thought. Although she could not be with the man her heart desired, and it might take time for her heart to accept that, it did not mean she was prepared to settle for a marriage of convenience. No, there would be plenty of time to marry. The first order of business was to survive the Season.

She was thankful that her aunt did not query it when she decided that she would stay in that evening instead of attending

Mrs. Fleming's dinner party. She had faith in her sisters' abilities to keep to their task and report back to her. Once everyone had departed, she took one stack of neatly folded and tied love letters out from the trunk and began to reread them.

Hours later, she was still reading the beautiful correspondence between her parents when her sisters entered the parlor.

"How did the evening progress?"

"Lord Grimsby and his cousin, Mr. Eastwick, were in attendance. Although the former kept to himself, did not join us for dinner, and departed early. It was as if he wanted to ensure his cousin didn't bolt. The poor fellow seemed nervous," Theodora said with empathy. "It was mentioned that this is Mr. Eastwick's first visit to Town. Lady Dorothy was also present and—"

"And Miss Jerome." The disdain in Evelina's voice was thick. "Thankfully, she was too consumed with herself to notice most around her. She announced that she's caught the eye of a gentleman and hopes to make an announcement soon. Why everyone hangs on her every word, I will never know."

"It's not because those around her like her. It's more likely because they are afraid of the poison she spews. No one, especially a young debutante trying to make a match, wants to be cast in an unfavorable light," Alexandra offered with the wisdom of an older sister.

"Once she's off the marriage market, she should be more tolerable, I suppose," Theodora commented.

"I highly doubt that. Aunt Imogene said Lady Jerome seems to get worse with age. I cannot imagine that her daughter will be any better," Evelina chimed in. "And let's not forget Mr. Rodney." Her sister let out a long huff of frustration. "He gets worse with each passing event. His boisterous tales of chivalry were most—"

Alexandra interrupted her sister's tirade, hoping to the turn conversation to something more pleasant. "I've been rereading our parents' letters." She handed one to Evelina. "This one is my favorite."

"It's a beautiful love poem," Evelina sighed with contentment. That was one of the positives about her. Annoyance with any topic or person usually did not last for long once poetry was involved.

Theodora rested her head on Evelina's shoulder and read the poem as well. "I miss them both so much," she said on a whisper.

Alexandra went to her sisters and brought them within her embrace. "As do I," she murmured as the words lodged in her throat.

"Me, too," Evelina said as she burst into tears, startling both her sisters. Alexandra pulled back and stared at her. It was unlike Evelina to give into such tears.

"What's wrong, dearest?"

"Nothing . . . I don't know . . . everything!"

What on earth had happened at the dinner party? Theodora caught her gaze and mouthed some words several times, but Alexandra struggled to guess what she was saying.

"Lord Raine!" Theodora huffed as she backed out of the embrace. "Evelina had words with Lord Raine. Really, Alexandra, you used to be so efficient at this—"

"Theodora Hera Grace, *that* man is not to be mentioned."

Alexandra and Theodora eyed their sister. Since her first encounter with Lord Raine, Evelina had been irritated, upset, disturbed, and altogether outraged whenever *that* man was present or even mentioned. No amount of poetry was going to ease the current situation.

Evelina threw up her hands and began to pace, airing her displeasure in the process. "Fine. I will tell you, but I will not speak *his* name," she stated with an air of absoluteness. "*That* man has to be without a doubt the rudest to ever walk the earth. He accused me—me!—of chasing after him, attempting to gain his attention, and . . ." She stopped, turned to face the sisters, then bellowed, "Of trying to seduce him."

"What happened—"

"I wasn't even trying to discover anything. I went to the

retiring room, and when I left to rejoin the ladies, he was there in the corridor, leaning casually against the wall as if waiting for someone. He claimed that I had followed him, and when I informed him of my utter disdain for someone of his ilk, he accused me of trying to seduce him."

"And what did you say?" Alexandra questioned.

"I informed him that if I *were* trying to seduce him, I would not be so coy as to sneak around in a dimly lit corridor, but would perform a bold act, leaving him and any one present with no doubt of my affections."

In her sister's current mood, Alexandra didn't know what she'd expected Evelina to say, but that certainly was not it.

"But it would ruin you," Theodora stated with concern.

Evelina's features were red and flushed with rage as she ranted. "But that's exactly why I said it, so *he* would comprehend how little I thought of *him*. I would never perform such an act, and I would certainly never do anything to satisfy the gossips."

Alexandra could not remember the last time she'd witnessed her sister in such a state of fury for any length of time. Certainly, she was dramatic at times, and she had a temper, but she never let anyone get the better of her. Alexandra could not help but wonder if there was more to the evening than Evelina was letting on. But now was not the time to delve into that. She would wait for her sister to calm down.

"It's getting late. You will feel better in the morning," she offered.

"I suppose," Evelina accepted with a huff, sounding more like a little girl of five who didn't want to go to bed than a grown woman of two and twenty. She went to her room without further words.

"Are you going to retire?" Alexandra questioned Theodora.

"No. I'm not tired." She caught Alexandra's eye, then added, "You needn't worry. I am not going to play the pianoforte in the middle of the night again."

"Poor Aunt Imogene's imagination hasn't yet recovered from

seeing you play in the wee, small hours of the morning, illuminated by moonlight."

"I still don't know why she thought I was a spirit come to haunt her." Theodora let out a sigh. "I wish we were back in the country and had the freedom to move about."

Alexandra was concerned about her youngest sister. Ever since their dearest papa had taken ill, and even after he'd passed away, Theodora had kept odd hours and wandered about the house and grounds. Alexandra had hoped with time it would improve, but Theodora's nighttime disquiet seemed worse than ever here in London. "I know, but we cannot change our current course." She brought her sister into her embrace. "Try to get some rest."

By the next morning, none of the three sisters were well rested, as evidenced by the dark circles under their eyes, and yet the sun still rose, and guests still arrived. Thankfully, no unwanted gossipy ladies darkened their doorstep that afternoon, so the attendees were free to discuss whatever was on their minds.

"I overheard my mother and Lady Archibald talking about Lord Grimsby's plans for a summer house party." Miss Ashton's mother was quite well connected and always seemed to have the most recent information on all activities within the *ton*. "It would appear that Lord Grimsby is frustrated with his cousin."

"Mr. Eastwick? Why? He seemed a pleasant fellow, albeit very shy," Theodora said.

"Do you know anything about him?" Miss Ashton questioned with interest, leading Alexandra to believe she might have formed a *tendre* for the gentleman. Perhaps all they needed was a little encouragement.

"We were paired together at Mrs. Fleming's dinner party. I thought him most sincere, once he had got past his nervousness, that is. We had a pleasant conversation about sailing."

"Oh, I do love being near water. When I was little, my father and I enjoyed skimming pebbles across its surface." The love in Miss Ashton's voice touched Alexandra's heart. Memories such as those were precious.

"Pardon me, Miss Grace," Roger started as he entered the room, "Lady Nerissa has just arrived."

No sooner had Roger announced the daughter of the duke, then she rushed into the room, excitement following on her hem. "I apologize for my late arrival."

Alexandra swallowed the hard lump that was edging its way up her throat. Guilt wrangled its way through her body as remembrances of the kiss she'd shared with Niall fought their way to the forefront of her mind. Why couldn't she simply forget that it had ever happened?

Because you've finally realized you're in love with him and you can never declare your feelings.

She shook those thoughts away and focused on their newest arrival. "Please join us. We will be having tea and—"

"I have an announcement," Lady Nerissa exclaimed with excitement.

Alexandra's stomach churned and her chest tightened. This was the moment she'd been dreading, the moment when their engagement would be made officially known. Her breath came in short spurts, spinning her world on its axis. She grabbed the edge of her chair to steady herself. *Smile and be happy for them.*

"But you have to promise not to say a word to anyone."

The ladies, practically on the edge of their seats, nodded their heads in unison.

"My mother will be furious when she discovers what I've done, but I do not care. I need to follow my heart." Lady Nerissa looked to Alexandra and her sisters. "I have you to thank for my current happiness." And then with a wide smile that revealed her nearly straight teeth, she announced, "Lord Jacobs has asked for my hand, and I've accepted," she ended on an excited squeal.

Alexandra's heart stopped for a moment before pounding back to life. Lady Nerissa and Niall weren't to marry? She took in a deep breath, then exhaled slowly, releasing the tension and anxiety that had been consuming her only a moment ago. She had not even contemplated what the news meant when, out of the corner of her eye, she spied her sisters' eyes upon her. Oh dear, what did they suspect?

"How wonderful!" Miss Raine offered as she went to their friend and embraced her. "He is quite an amiable gentleman."

"Since we're making announcements," Lady Dorothy said as she stood, "Mr. Greenford and I are engaged."

Once again, Alexandra was rendered speechless. Thankfully, Theodora asked the question that was on her mind. "Isn't he a fortune hunter?"

"He *is* in need of funds, but not because of his mismanagement. His father left a mountain of debt and the estate in near ruins."

"But he boasted about the recent renovations," Evelina said as she shook her head.

"Because he thought that's what a lady would want to hear. He has begun to turn things around but of course it takes money. Before he declared his intentions, he was honest about the state of his home and finances. My father was not too keen on the match at first, but Mr. Greenford has been asking for his advice and talking to him about improvements. My father always wanted a son and the two have become very close."

"Are you certain he is all that he claims to be?" Evelina's question was thick with doubt.

Had they been wrong in their assumptions of other gentlemen?

Alexandra was about to pose her question when Lady Dorothy responded, "Yes, and more. He is quite romantic and the kiss we shared was perfect," she ended with a dreamy sigh.

The declaration took Alexandra back to that glorious moment when Niall had kissed her. She knew the feeling all too well. Now that Lady Nerissa was promised to another, what did it mean for her and Niall? Hope soared through her veins. Perhaps . . .

As usual, once the ladies took their leave, the three sisters retreated to their private parlor to talk about the events of the afternoon. Alexandra's head was spinning from all the news that had been announced, but her mind was still centered on one person. Niall.

She had no clue as to what she should do. Should she wait for him to come to her? Or should she go to him and tell him how she felt? What if he didn't feel the same? He'd confessed that he'd always wanted to kiss her, but that didn't necessarily mean that he was in love with her. If she'd learnt anything this Season, it was that physical attraction did not equal love.

She slumped in the chair beside the fireplace trying to sort through all the questions storming her mind, when Theodora blurted out, "Why didn't you tell us Lady Nerissa was promised to Niall?"

Alexandra bolted upright, completely stunned. "How did you guess who it was? Lady Nerissa did not say who she was promised to and—"

"I saw the look on your face when Lady Nerissa announced it was Lord Jacobs."

"You can't keep secrets from us. We know you too well. We know each other too well," Evelina said.

Alexandra worried her hands, feeling horrible for deceiving her sisters. "I should have told you, but I made a promise to Niall. Can you ever forgive me?"

"You have nothing to be sorry for, but always know that we're here for you," Evelina said with tenderness.

"For each other," Theodora reinforced the sentiment. "Now, what did you promise Niall?"

Alexandra chuckled. She should have known that since Lady Nerissa's secret was mostly out in the open, her sisters would be full of questions. "Years ago, he confided that his family and the

Duchess of Harewood arranged for their children to marry."

"Why did he agree?"

"I don't think he had much say in the arrangement. He was just a young lad at the time. Plus, you know how the dowager duchess can be once she sets her mind to something." Over the years, the formidable woman had caused many a woe with her incessant behavior regarding everything from the trees that bordered their property in the country, to the balls she'd hosted where the sisters did not attend due to their mother's illness. It seemed as if the dowager was always enraged by something or someone.

"She is a master of guilt." Theodora tsked several times. "I understand why Mother never cared for her. Although I do wonder why she never cared for us?"

"Perhaps she suspected Alexandra's feelings for her son," Evelina stated matter-of-factly.

Alexandra was speechless. How did her sisters know when she'd only recently discovered her feelings for Niall?

"You needn't look so shocked, Alexandra," Evelina said. "Even when you were oblivious to the obvious, Theodora and I would discuss when you would finally realize it."

"How . . . how long have you known?"

Theodora blinked several times as if doing the calculations in her head. "At least three years."

"Three years?" Had she really been that unaware of her own feelings for *that long*? "How did—"

"We know?" Evelina finished her question. "One would have had to been blind not see how he looked at you, and you him."

"And hard of hearing not to notice the concern in his voice for you after Mother, then Papa, died," Theodora added. "You were always the first person he asked about." She placed a gentle hand on hers. "The question now remains, when will you go to him and confess *your* feelings?"

Chapter Twelve

I T HAD BEEN several days since he'd seen Alexandra, pressed against the wall, hiding behind a pedestal. She had looked so sad, so miserable. He'd wanted nothing more than to cross the room and comfort her. The Season would soon be at an end, and his mother fully expected an announcement to be made. This was to be the last ball he would attend as an unattached gentleman.

He watched the couples on the dance floor, each trying to impress the other in the marriage mart game. With only a few weeks left of the Season, it seemed as if there was panic in the air amongst those who'd yet to secure a proposal. Even Naomi was anxious about the outcome of the Season, not because Niall was pressuring her, but because their mother was. Mother had narrowed down her list of suitable gentlemen—from those of good family and fortune, "worthy enough to marry her youngest daughter." Niall had had to refrain from laughter when his mother had spoken those words on their journey here. Mother was not concerned for anything, save her own reputation and social standing. He'd bowed to her demands for his own choice—or lack thereof—of bride, but he certainly wouldn't force his sister to do the same. He would stand his ground and endure the dowager's wrath.

As the music faded and the couples returned to their respective parties, Lady Nerissa rushed past Niall and whispered, "I must speak with you immediately."

His gaze followed the direction in which she was briskly walking. The brown-haired beauty looked over her shoulder, then nodded toward a side corridor, indicating that she wanted him to go in that direction.

He didn't know what was so pressing that she couldn't wait until a more appropriate time. It was quite out of the ordinary, although perhaps that was appropriate considering the past week. He made his way toward the corridor, ensuring no prying eyes were following, or worse, his mother.

"*Pst! Pst!* Over here." He heard Lady Nerissa call to him from a side room in hushed tones.

Propriety dictated that he not follow her into the partially darkened room. If they were discovered . . . well, it wouldn't be any different than the situation he currently found himself in. Their engagement was to be announced two days hence at the extravagant ball her mother was hosting. At this point, he had nothing to lose. Shaking his head, he stepped into the room that was lit by a single candle. A moment later, she closed the door.

"What is so pressing? This is highly inappropriate—"

"I don't want to marry you," she blurted out. He thought he'd misheard her and was about to ask for clarification when she repeated, "I cannot marry you. I'm terribly sorry." Her face was concealed by shadows, but her words were firm and confident, without a hint of sadness. "I'm certain my mother will not be pleased with my choice, but if I have learned anything from the three Grace sisters, it is to follow my heart."

Slowly, the words penetrated his brain, and he formed them into a cohesive sentence. *She didn't want to marry him.*

His silence must have alarmed her. She then added quickly, "And my heart belongs to Lord Jacobs. I hope you understand."

"Completely." Relief coursed through his body. "I don't know what to say."

"You don't need to say anything. We would never have suited, although I suspect we both would have made the best of it."

"I was prepared to. I would never have done anything to dishonor you." He meant every word. He would never do anything to disgrace the woman he married, even if it was not a love match.

"I know you wouldn't have, and I thank you for that. But I think we both deserve a chance at happiness . . . and love."

Wise words from someone so young. If only Society were driven by love, kindness, and respect, then the world would be a better place. Sadly, many would not know love or anything like it. There were too many marriages purely made for the advancement of rank, wealth, and lineage.

She took a step closer and out of the shadows. "And I think . . ." There was a long pause before she continued. "I think there is a remarkable lady who's been aiding her friends in finding true love who has caught your eye."

He'd been most careful over the years about burying any attachment for Alexandra. Had he somehow revealed his feelings? Did others suspect?

He was just about to ask when Lady Nerissa said with a sincere smile, "I wish you much happiness, Your Grace."

"And I wish you many happy years with Lord Jacobs. He's a fine fellow." And he was. He was certain that the young baron would do everything within his reach to ensure this daughter of a duke lived the life she hoped for and wanted for nothing.

"Thank you." Then, without any delay, Lady Nerissa took her leave.

Niall had been handed a chance at happiness he'd hardly dared hope for and did not want to waste another moment. And yet, he didn't want the gossips to notice that he and Lady Nerissa had been gone at the same time and then returned to the ballroom within minutes of each other. He did not want to endure the censure of their wagging tongues. The worst, by far, was Lady Shepard.

An agonizing quarter of an hour passed before he made his

escape in search of Alexandra. However, no sooner had he entered the refreshment hall than his mother stormed to his side.

Do not let her get the better of you.

"I've just received the most alarming news," she started on a hiss. "Lady Nerissa was seen, not even ten minutes ago, sneaking off with Lord Jacobs."

News certainly traveled swiftly. "How did you . . ."

"You know something." Her gaze bore down on him, assessing him. "What have you learned?"

"It doesn't matter what I know. What matters is that Lady Nerissa is happy—"

"And is disgracing her family with a baron!" Mother's voice ricocheted through the room, startling those near to them. "All our plans were for what? You should have announced your engagement and—"

"And then? I'd have been miserable like you and Father?" He shook his head. "This is not the time or place to be having this discussion."

Mother had already been the subject of the gossips earlier in the Season when she'd lost her temper over Mr. Norley and Naomi having lemonade. Clearly she did not want that to happen again. Appearances were important to her, and she would rather keep her mouth shut tight and let her anger build than allow anyone to see her in distress . . . again.

She pasted on a wide smile, sucked in her breath, and strolled away as if nothing unpleasant—unpleasant in her mind, at least— had occurred.

He spent the next hour searching the ballroom, refreshment hall, and card room for Alexandra, but she was nowhere to be found. Even her sisters had disappeared from the event. For a brief moment, he thought about going to Lady Middleton's home, but the hour was late, and despite everything, he was a gentleman and acutely aware of how precarious his situation was. Even though there had never been a formal announcement about him and Lady Nerissa, he was very much connected to her family. He could not care less what the rumormongers said about him, but he had to consider Naomi. His sister was enjoying this first Season and he would not do anything to diminish her happiness or subjugate her to gossips.

Hours later, he was finally trudging up the grand staircase of his ducal townhouse to his suite of rooms. Upon his arrival home, Horace, their butler, had informed him that the Dowager Duchess had retired with heavy dose of laudanum, but not before yelling her displeasure about the world to the entire household. And that was precisely why Niall had gone to his club after the ball and not returned home with his family. He'd had enough of her lectures and antics for one night.

All he wanted to do was change out of his evening attire, have a glass of brandy, and determine his next course of action. As he entered his suite and then closed the door, the faint scent of vanilla drifted past him, reminding him of—

"Alexandra."

ALEXANDRA DIDN'T CARE if what she was doing was inappropriate. After Lady Nerissa had confided in the ladies of the salon earlier that afternoon and told them that she could not marry the man her parents wanted her to, that she was going to follow her heart and elope to Gretna Green with Lord Jacobs, all Alexandra could think about was confessing her feelings to Niall.

With the aid of her sisters, she'd concocted a plan to be seen at the evening's ball, then would quickly return home and change into her men's attire and sneak into Niall's home. What she needed to say had to be done in private, not at some event where the loose-lipped lurked and she could lose her nerve.

She had donned her brother's clothing once more and snuck out of her aunt's home. Only this time she wasn't attending an illicit masque or venturing into one of London's notorious gaming hells in search of answers. No, tonight she was going to take a chance on love.

She traveled through the night, keeping to the shadows. Niall's house wasn't far, but it simply would not do to be discovered now, not after all the creeping around she'd done without being caught. This journey was more important than all the other escapades combined.

Her breathing quickened as she neared the ducal townhouse, revealing the coolness of the night in white puffy clouds. It was already quite late, and most of the servants should have retired, but she wasn't taking any chances. She watched for movement through the ground floor windows, but there was no activity. Satisfied that her earlier assumption was correct, she went around to the rear servants' entrance.

Soon she was winding her way up the servants' stairwell. She opened the door on the family floor and was instantly met with the sound of the dowager's wails and complaints.

"I cannot believe the daughter of a duke would choose a baron over a duke!" Her cry echoed down the corridor. Alexandra knew that the dowager was referring to Lady Nerissa. However, she truly wished the best for both Lord Jacobs and Nerissa as, in her estimation, the pair made a lovely couple. "Bring me laudanum!" Another wail reverberated from somewhere deeper in the house.

Alexandra counted to twenty, then eased the door open and peered around. She let out a long sigh. No one was in sight. Now was her opportunity. She edged out from her hiding place and started her search for Niall's room. From a comment that Naomi had made, she knew that the dowager duchess's rooms were at the opposite end of the house from those of her children, and she was certain that Niall's room was in this wing.

The search did not take long. The moment she opened the second door, she was met with an earthy scent.

Books.

Without a doubt, this had to be Niall's chamber. Upon entering the suite, she slunk from behind the sofa to the chair, just in case his valet was present. The soft, warm glow from the fireplace created shadows, concealing her presence. Once certain she was alone, she took off the hat and coat that hid her identity, then took the opportunity to look about the set of rooms.

They were very much like Niall, neat and tidy. Then her gaze drifted to a large writing desk with papers strewn across its surface. She looked at the various drawings, some done in precise detail while others appeared to have been sketched with a more relaxed hand. There was something sensual about those images, something personal, something—.

"Alexandra," Niall's deep, husky voice sent a ripple of desire through her body.

She turned around to face him. His features were cast in shadow, making it difficult to read his reaction to her presence. "Before you say anything or reprimand me for sneaking in here, or tell me how inappropriate I'm being, I wanted . . . that is to say . . ." Confessing one's feelings was more difficult than she thought it would be. She took in a long deep breath to steady her nerves then blurted out what she'd been wanting to say before common sense took over. "I love you. I think I always have. You are my closest friend, the person I want to spend my days and nights with, to build a life with."

One moment she was confessing her feelings, the next she was in his arms, his mouth on hers, telling her without words that she was loved. She'd found what she'd been searching for this Season—no, her whole adult life.

She laced her fingers through his silky hair, bringing him closer to her, wanting so much yet not knowing how to ask for what she wanted. He shifted the angle of his head, the spectacles he wore pressing against her cheek. She pulled back and looked into his green eyes, deep with hunger and desire.

Alexandra reached for his spectacles, "Do you need these?"

"Not as much as I claim to."

To say she was confused was an understatement. The women

of her acquaintance who wore eyeglasses were degraded by the perception of what it meant to wear them. Did only women suffer this affliction? "Why would you pretend to need them?"

He removed the spectacles and placed them on an obliging side table. He then brought her back into his embrace and rested his forehead against hers. "They helped me feel safe. I've never let anyone see me without them. It was easier to hide behind them, protecting who I truly was."

"Who you truly were?" His admission caught her off guard.

"I enjoy reading dissertations on architecture and farming rather than hunting or watching a fight. I prefer the quiet solitude of an evening spent at home to attending the latest ball or soirée. You once said I was like a Doric column, neat and tidy, and classically understated, which is one step away from dull."

"I see *you*, and you are without a doubt *not* dull."

"I'm not?" She heard the challenge in his voice and accepted it.

"You are passionate." She brushed a soft kiss to the corner of his eye, then trailed her lips across his smooth cheek and whispered in his ear, "And I suspect you have many hidden desires."

It was as if her words inflamed him. One hand smoothed down her back, cradling her bottom, bringing her closer into his hardness, while the other worked to remove clothing. One by one, their garments fell until they stood naked before each other. His eyes glittered with desire—desire for her.

"Thank you for letting me see you without your spectacles."

"Thank you for seeing me."

She took a step closer, not just wanting to see but to feel and explore. Her fingers roamed over his smooth, muscular chest, then traveled downward toward his manhood. She'd never imagined a man could be so perfectly formed. She'd known Niall most of her life and yet never dreamed he looked like this. He was a Corinthian, indeed. His breath grew ragged as she continued her exploration. She wrapped her hand around his erection, feeling him grow harder in her hands.

"Alexandra," he growled her name as he whisked her into his arms then took her to the bed.

His mouth trailed along her collarbone to the hollow of her throat then wandered down her chest. With each kiss, her heart beat faster and her body yearned for more. And when he took one hard bud in his mouth, sucking at the tip, she gasped in pleasure then begged for more.

"I want you, Niall. I want to feel you, all of you."

He shifted his body, covering hers with his warmth. "This may hurt," he said with such tenderness that her heart practically wept. Then, in one swift thrust, he was inside her.

She sucked in her breath as pain stabbed her, replacing the pleasure of moments ago. But, just as quickly, it subsided. He brushed tender kisses across her lips, his body remaining still as she adjusted to him.

Feeling bolder, she flicked her tongue across his lips. It was the only encouragement he needed. In the next breath, he'd taken her mouth in a heated, passionate kiss that made her toes curl. Hearts beating, bodies melding, they moved as one.

Her body was awash in a tide of pleasure, as sensations she'd never thought possible flowed through her, tumbling waves upon the shore. Niall was gentle and caring, bringing her pleasure she'd never imagined. This was the passion she'd been searching for.

A cry tore from her lips as she found her release. A moment later, a hoarse groan escaped his lips, then, keeping her within his arms, he rolled onto his back.

Alexandra could think of no place else she would rather be than wrapped in Niall's embrace. She kissed his smooth chest, inhaling his scent that reminded her of reading a book on a chilly day.

"I love you with all my heart, Alex."

She raised herself up and stared into his beautiful green eyes. "Does this mean you will you marry me, Your Grace?"

"It's most improper of you to ask," he teased then took her

mouth in a deep, sensual kiss. "Only if you continue to be a most improper duchess," he said in a husky tone that sent her pulse racing anew.

"That I can." She rolled on top of him. "There are desires I wish to explore with only you, Your Grace. Each and every day."

JUST BEFORE DAWN, and before the sun began to make its presence known to the world, Niall dressed a reluctant Alexandra and escorted her back to Lady Middleton's home. As he returned to his residence, his thoughts centered on the many changes that had occurred over the past few days. He had waited a lifetime to have Alexandra in his arms, and he would not tarry a day longer. Today, he would secure a special license, then inform his mother of his decision.

Hours later, with his business concluded, his mother had only just emerged into the day parlor. Her mood was no better than it had been the night before.

"I have sent word to Her Grace informing her I wish to discuss Lady Nerissa. We will get—"

"Mother, I have secured a special license."

The dowager's eyes lit up, and a wide smile forced her cheeks upward. "Lady Nerissa has come to her senses."

"In fact, she has." He realized he was taunting the dragon, but he didn't care. "She is to marry Lord Jacobs and—"

"But you secured—"

"A special license for me and my bride." He paused, using his mother's tactic for dramatic suspense. "Miss Alexandra Grace." He braced himself for the hysterics that were certain to come.

A moment later, they did.

His mother pushed back from the table then stood with force, knocking the chair over. Her deep crimson cheeks filled with rage burned as fiery words lashed from her mouth. "I forbid it!" She bellowed. "You will not marry that . . . that . . ."

"You have no say," he calmly stated. "It is all arranged."

He did not wait for her response but strolled from the room, in control of his life. He could hear her wails and cries as he emerged into the bright day. For the first time in his life, he felt refreshed without the weight of responsibility bearing down on him. Being a duke meant he had numerous duties, but he'd realized those never really bothered him. It was the demands of his mother that had been dragging him through the murky depths of barely existing. With the woman he'd always loved soon to be at his side as his wife, his duchess, anything seemed possible.

SEVERAL DAYS LATER, under a cloudy sky that threatened rain, and surrounded by their closest family, Niall and Alexandra became husband and wife. Afterward, they returned to Lady Middleton's home for the wedding breakfast. It was a joyous day surrounded by those Niall cared most about. Even his mother had managed to paste on a tolerable smile for the event. He hoped with time she would come to terms with his decision and embrace her new daughter-in-law. Something deep down told him the dowager was not capable of such affection, but he could hope.

It seemed as if most of the *ton* attended the wedding breakfast too. Much to his annoyance, he didn't have even five minutes alone with his bride. He counted down the minutes, then seconds, till they could depart and he could finally have her all to himself.

His estimation was drastically wrong.

Hours later, they were finally ensconced in the ducal carriage, journeying through London, attempting to make their escape to the country. He could not wait until they were truly alone. He wanted nothing more than to take her clothes off and worship her.

"I think I know what you're thinking, Your Grace," she said in a seductive tone that sent his pulse racing.

He pulled her across the seat and onto his lap. "And what am I thinking, Your Grace?" he said, then plundered her mouth with a long, seductive kiss.

"Yes," she purred, as she ran her fingers through his hair. One hand then traveled down his chest, edging further and further down. "Just what I thought."

"You *are* a most improper duchess."

Epilogue

ALEXANDRA STROLLED THROUGH the rose garden, relishing the cool early autumn. She inhaled the earthy scents of nature. Soon, the leaves would start to change color and the landscape would take on a new identity. She was looking forward to experiencing Blackburn Hall in each season. Although she'd visited the estate numerous times, this was now her home. From the classical colonnade to the wide staircase that curved three stories tall, to the intimate private rooms she shared with her husband and the sweeping views that took her breath away, this was where she would build a life with her love.

She continued farther down the path toward the hedge maze. Remembrances of childhood jaunts through the one at her family's home tickled her mind. Many happy memories had been made there and she hoped she could bring the same joy and wonder to this place.

"I thought I would find you here," her husband's deep voice called to her, sending those delicious tingles she reveled in so much down her body.

She turned around, expecting to see him smiling back, but even through his spectacles, she could see the worry lines creasing the corners of his eyes.

She was just about to ask if something was the matter when

he waved a letter and said, "It would seem that the Three Graces' Salon has struck again."

Oh no! She swallowed hard. "Who—"

"My sister." He closed the distance between them, brought her into his embrace and kissed her lips with such passion that she thought she might swoon. The kiss slowed and he rested his forehead against hers. "She followed her heart and eloped with Nathaniel Norley, and I have you to thank for that."

"You're not angry?"

"No." He brushed a kiss across her cheek. "Relieved actually. My mother on the other hand . . ." He shook his head several times. "Upon hearing the news, she informed me that, despite Mr. Norley's surname beginning with the letter *N*, she did not approve. She is disowning me and Naomi, will not be living in any house that I reside in, and instead will be spending her remaining days with my eldest sister, who, according to her, does what she's told and never causes any trouble. She has already called for her carriage and insists on departing within the hour."

Oh heavens, but her mother-in-law was certainly one for dramatics. Alexandra had met Niall's sister Nelly on several occasions. She suspected mother and daughter had much in common. She did feel sorry for her brother-in-law though. He seemed a pleasant fellow. "A lot of changes are on the horizon. I wish her much happiness then."

"I don't believe my mother is capable of any happiness." He brought her within his embrace once again. "I believe that's enough change for now," he playfully said as he teased her lips.

"Well, not quite." Alexandra pulled away, nibbling her bottom lip for a moment. She had waited until she was absolutely certain . . . and she was. "At least we have some months to prepare for this next little change."

The spot between Niall's brows crinkled as he worked out the meaning of her words, then all of a sudden, his features relaxed and his lovely green eyes sparkled with sheer joy. He brushed his hand across her still flat stomach. "We're going to have a baby?"

She nodded her head. "The first of many."

Of course, one of her fondest dreams had always been to have a large, happy family of her own with the man she loved and desired by her side.

Dreams did come true.

About the Author

Bestselling, award-winning author, Alanna Lucas pens Regency-set historicals filled with romance, adventure, and of course, happily ever afters. When she is not daydreaming of her next travel destination, Alanna can be found researching, spending time with family, tending to her garden, or going for long walks. She makes her home in California with her husband and children, and too many books to count.

Just for the record, you can never have too many handbags or books. And travel is a must.

www.ingramcontent.com/pod-product-compliance
Lightning Source LLC
Chambersburg PA
CBHW071941190726
48293CB00004B/1305